The Island of Zoe

Dino Hajiyorgi
& Christos Sourligas

THE ISLAND OF ZOE
Copyright © 2023 by Dino Hajiyorgi & Christos Sourligas

ISBN: 979-8-88653-142-8

Published by Satin Romance
An Imprint of Melange Books, LLC
White Bear Lake, MN 55110
www.satinromance.com

Published in the United States of America.

Cover Design by Caroline Andrus

CONTENTS

For Dino

MAIN CHARACTERS

Zoe — Early 30s, Greek American female, clothing store owner. Zoe is toned from her daily yoga sessions, stylishly-dressed, olive-skinned, has a sparkle in her eye. She's over-worked, burnt out from city life, and ready to connect with the simple island way of living.

Sophia — Hawkish, conservative and controlling elderly woman, she carries the island's weight on her shoulders. Her main goal is to send Zoe packing before the island's secrets are revealed.

Rita — Petite, elderly Greek widow, dressed in the traditional black. Rita has the spring in her step of someone 30 years younger — and a sunny smile to match!

Stefanos — Tall, dapper, serious elderly man, but with the physique and agility of someone quite a bit younger. Stefanos is Zoe's grandmother (Maria) former lover.

Maria — Devoted, proud, and hard-working, she stops at nothing to get what she wants. Zoe's grandmother and true inspiration, Maria's life story is told mainly through flashbacks.

Paris — 40-year-old, dark and handsome watchmaker, and a Greek priest-in-training. His 5 o'clock shadow high-lights his sea blue eyes. An introvert, he plays by his own rules.

Father Michael — Paris' father, also a priest, bearded in the Greek orthodox style. He exudes positivity, faith and patience.

Claudia — German geologist, serious, and studious. Claudia's in her mid-30s and slightly tomboyish. She prefers the company of animals and birds to most people, but has a soft spot for Zoe.

Manos — Fun, good-natured bon vivant who runs the island's only store.

ONE
PETRA

"Ekaterini mou!" (*My Ekaterini!*)

She burst her eyes open and shook off the cobwebs of her jetlag. The echo of her grandmother's voice—her *Yiayia*—lingered a little while longer before it turned into cries of seagulls. "Had she dozed off on her feet? That would be embarrassing in front of all these strangers," she thought. All the same, her only job now was to tightly fasten her hands on her hips and heavily balance her feet on this small but fast-moving boat. It seemed like a dream that just forty-eight hours ago she was frantically hailing a cab on West 29th Street. And here she was, now being greeted by an incredible assortment of blue hues found only in picture postcards. She brushed her windblown locks away from her face to take it all in.

The island of Petra was coming up ahead, and it was beginning to shed its cloak, awash by the most magical sunlight. Framed by sky and sea, it flaunted its prehistoric mounds of mountains with spotted dots of red-tiled rooftops, which made up for the island's significant lack of flora. Miles away from shore, the faint bell of a church managed to reach her ears, and yet, there was no lamentation in its toll. If anything, it was a welcoming call of celebration.

Zoe drew in a deep breath and felt the fragrant salt air pleasantly sting her senses. She happily shut her eyes this time, but not to catch some sleep. Zoe was living the life of two people now, and in this state of profound absorption, she was finally using the breathing exercises she had learned in yoga class.

After an awkward minute or so, she slowly opened her eyes and looked about the bow, wondering if her free-standing catnaps were being monitored. Two Hellenic Navy Seamen and Mr. Kanakis, the public official, were anxiously gazing at their destination completely oblivious of her concern. Her Mediterranean beauty looked doubly striking in her New York-style fashions. A tad worn out by her journey so far, Zoe felt anything but polished. Her jeans, boots, jersey and leather jacket now laid heavily on her.

Wiping the seawater and sweat from her brow, she hoped there would be a hot shower waiting for her somewhere at the end of all this. It would be the completion of a granddaughter's duty, as her father had put it.

Her eyes rested on the silver coffin at the feet of the navy guards. She knew it was Grandma's voice that had stirred her out of her sleep. But who was this "Ekaterini" that Grandma called out for? It had been an arduous trek, with all the hassle of paperwork from the Greek Consulate in New York to the airport in Athens, and more red tape on the main island of Andoriani; this archipelago's municipality unit.

Zoe felt some of her jetlag being washed away by this miraculous sea breeze. "Are you still talking to me, Yiayia?" she thought. "Here we are... you're finally back home."

Zoe looked at the island, its details emerging even clearer now. This was her grandmother Maria's home, the ancestral island of Petra. Yiayia never talked about her life in Greece. She never shared stories of the island with her granddaughter. Still, Zoe couldn't shake her gut feeling that she was about to embark on a voyage of discoveries, that she would encounter countless lost secrets along the way. And she knew exactly the kinds. The ones that lay hidden deep inside the family trunk, hoping never to be found.

Yiayia and Zoe had a falling out during the last few years, and Maria was mostly a stranger to Zoe by the time she was summoned to New York Presbyterian a month ago. In palliative care, she met an unrecognizable shrunken old lady, a shadow of the icon that Zoe had fondly remembered. Yiayia Maria barely spoke a word in her dying moments. Then, "Take me home... take me to Petra," she uttered with her dying breath. And here they were together, the granddaughter honoring her Yiayia's dying wish.

It took a while to figure out where Petra was. Even Zoe's mom, who was born in America, had no real stories of Greece to tell. All of it had to be quickly researched and googled. She even swallowed lots of pride and asked her father for money for the trip; a plane ticket for herself, and shipping expenses and all, for the deceased. This one sacred obligation—to be buried in one's homeland—her dad completely understood, despite his long disconnection from his very own Greek heritage. Zoe never thought of herself as a Greek, as a... *romantic*. Proof she was thirty years old, and this was the first time in her life that she had stepped on Greek soil. And somehow, this unfolding scenery seemed to be inviting her in like a welcoming nod —a sensation both foreign and familiar—which she could not explain. And somehow it had Yiayia Maria written all over it.

Closer to the island, Zoe noticed an even bigger navy boat patrolling the waters. Zoe had seen a similar vessel docked at the harbor of Andoriani only thirty minutes before.

"The navy seems to be everywhere," she commented to Mr. Kanakis, drawing his attention.

"Illegal migrants are an issue these days. We have had some *troubles*, but not anywhere near here," he answered. For some reason, Mr. Kanakis didn't sound very convincing. He graciously turned away from Zoe, brushing off her stare.

What Google had spilled out about Petra, apart from the usual tourist information—history, traditions, points of interest—were the claims that it was considered a Blue Zone. Meaning it was one of those magical places where people can easily live for a hundred years and up. And there were only five other Blue Zones on the planet, according to anecdotal evidence that had led to research studies which included Icaria, also in Greece, Sardinia, Okinawa, Nicoya in Costa Rica, and Loma Linda, California.

These places were known for their low cancer rates, barely any heart disease and almost no dementia. The common thread, as several studies had concluded, the populations of Blue Zone regions were family-oriented, highly socially engaged people and semi-vegetarians who practiced daily physical activity.

She also discovered a rather unpleasant footnote in the history of Petra from World War II. It had been a German outpost and the site of a horrible Nazi atrocity. Thirty-three unarmed islanders had been rounded up and executed as a reprisal to the killing of just one Wehrmacht soldier. Other than those two facts, Zoe knew nothing about Petra.

Zoe had been to Europe before, backpacking through Italy and France with her high school besties just after graduation. And once, she travelled through the remote Baja Peninsula in Mexico with an ex-boyfriend. So she had some experience with adventure travel, and in her mind, she was ready for this trip. But all she knew of Greece was from a few movies and series she had watched as a teen while lounging on the sofa and binging-watching AMC, HBO and Showtime classics. And on occasion when Grandma would visit them in Saratoga Springs, New York, Zoe welcomed the out of the blue live commentaries from Yiayia as they viewed together.

One in particular was called "Mediterraneo", which told the story of a group of young Italian soldiers that got washed up on a Greek island after Allied troops had sunk their ship. Zoe had such fond memories of the film, not so much of its content, but more for her grandmother's ear-to-ear smile as she gazed at the tube in jaw-dropping awe. And after the movie had ended, Yiayia wiped away her tears and immediately retorted, "Phooey romantic drivel. A typical, romanticized portrayal of Greeks by clueless non-Greek filmmakers." She then got up, headed straight to the liquor cabinet and helped herself to a stiff drink.

"Small-minded, petty, stubborn hotheads, that's what they really are," Yiayia Maria went on to say, pointing her finger to Zoe. "Now you marry a nice American boy who will treat you like a queen, you hear me?" Zoe lovingly burst out laughing. And yet, she was now in a Hollywood movie, herself the protagonist, as her boat began to dock at Petra.

"Yiayia, am I a *real* Greek?" she had asked back then.

"Fat chance!" her mother shouted from the next room.

The jab was clearly aimed at Yiayia, of course. Zoe had witnessed a fair share of power struggles between the two of them. But Maria's thick skin didn't care much for her daughter's retorts. Maria just thumbed her nose at her daughter and leaned in closer to Zoe's ear and whispered, "That, of course you are, sweetie. You'll always be Greek. Your children will be too... I just know it."

Under a canopy of white, blue and ochre-colored houses, a cast of Greek characters started to fill the island's harbor. There were hundreds of them, all looking at Zoe; lined up like a tragic chorus on a stage, ready to lament dramatic words for the arrival of one of their own. They were a surprising array of mainly old and wrinkled faces. Women in black, and men in dark suits with the traditional black mourning armbands tightly wrapped around their garbed biceps. She felt rather awkward for being at the center of so much attention. Additional navy personnel stood on the dock anxiously waiting alongside the islanders.

As the boat kissed the dock, the seaman quickly secured the craft by the bollards before climbing aboard to help with the coffin. The islanders gathered closer on the pier in anticipation. Zoe could not help but stare at their faces. Their ages ranged from seventy to ninety, yet there was an eager, youthful sparkle in their eyes and glowing faces. It was as if they were actually greeting Maria instead, the crowd weirdly hoping she would startle everyone and step onto the island alive, descending the boat in her high heels, wearing her Coco Chanel dress, her long pearl necklace, her fox fur hanging from her shoulders, waving her gloved hands at them like a royal. Wouldn't that be something?

The crowd's eyes were fixed on the coffin, some gratefully smiled, while others kept a mere grieving disposition. All hands were on deck as everyone labored to hand the coffin over to the island, a precarious moment as the boat bobbed on frisky waves.

Zoe felt a sudden rush of alarm. She outstretched her

arms to offer up assistance, but it was too little too late. Just as her instinct had predicted, a navy seaman tripped up, sending the coffin angling sideways and dragging the remaining pallbearers, nearly dropping the whole lot into the sea. A loud gasp rocketed out of the crowd. Was the casket lid securely fastened? Overcome with dread, Zoe let out a scream as she envisioned the indignity of her grand-mother's shriveled up body slipping out and being dumped out like a lifeless crash test dummy.

"Yiayia!" she yelled in terror. The pallbearers wobbled, their knees buckled. It was an imminent disaster; a fall, a crash onto the pier, a tumble to the sea? *Oh God, no!* Zoe shrilled to herself.

A tall silhouette sprang from the throng of elders and darted toward the boat. His broad shoulders and equally strong-arms grabbed the coffin and lifted it securely back to the pallbearers. Shocked, Zoe turned and looked at this man who had appeared like an angel. Or was he a hero in some romance novel simply helping out a damsel in distress? Her very own Greek Prince William? All she knew was that he seemingly didn't belong to this crew of golden-aged islanders. Complemented by a hipster beard, distinguished cheekbones and a strong chin, the stranger's deep blue eyes stared at her reassuringly.

"There, all secured. No harm done," he stressed, with a hint of a smile.

"Thank you," she stammered, as she felt hot blood flushing through her cheeks. Was her mouth agape the whole time, she wondered, totally embarrassed?

Once the coffin was safely laid onto the surface of the pier, the young hero then turned his helping hand to Zoe. She noticed he was wearing a gray vestment, like the kind churchy folk wear.

"Thank you," she repeated, feeling shy like a schoolgirl.

As she was aided off the boat, her face kept burning. She just hated losing control and feeling helpless, especially when meeting people for the very first time. Zoe worked in sales back home and she took pride in keeping her shit together. As she glanced over to her grandma's coffin for assurance, she chuckled. The apple never really falls far from the tree, she concluded. Zoe surely got her firebrand temperament from her Yiayia, and this epiphany made her feel rock solid. Just then, she knew she had to be here. Her grandma and her, now sharing the stage with a chorus of strangers.

The tapestry of islanders edged forward like a dawdling wave and in no time Zoe was surrounded. She barely spoke a word of Greek and tried to think of something to say. Anything, even in English would be preferable to standing tongue-tied as she was now.

This very moment had been an anxious one—one she meditated on it during her flight from New York City. She didn't sleep a wink, obsessing on what awaited her at the end of her journey. Yiayia Maria had spoken very little of Greece, let alone of Petra. Even despite the fact she had baptized Zoe's mom with an imitative of that name... Patra. Short for Cleopatra, which Zoe learned later on in life meant "glory of the father". But she never really understood the real meaning behind it; at least the personal reasoning for Grandma to have named her one and only child that way.

And how could Zoe have imagined, years later, that she would be visiting an isolated Greek island and meeting all its inhabitants who now devoured her with their eyes, expecting her to say something wise in Greek? She thought of saying to Mr. Kanakis, "I have no speech prepared," hoping he would help out with a quick and easy translation, and in turn, a forgiving response from the elderly crowd. Out of nowhere, an Orthodox priest stepped out of the crowd and approached her with his hand extended. Dressed all in black, he looked to be in his mid-fifties, with a friendly, reassuring face underlined by a thick, gray beard.

"Welcome to Petra," he said in perfect English, shaking her hand. "I'm Father Michael," he continued with a warm smile. "On behalf of the entire island, I would like to extend our deepest sympathies for your loss."

"Thank you, Father. Happy to be here, all things considered," she quickly replied, letting out a deep breath, finally feeling some relief.

"Your grandmother Maria was a vital part of our community... and of our history," added the priest.

"Really? I had no idea, Father," Zoe said, nodding with a polite smile.

"We are all family here, so you're in good hands. Come, let's meet the others," he motioned.

The islanders had closed a tight circle around them, attentively listening to their every word. They extended their hands, touching Zoe reassuringly with soft pats and taps, giving her their condolences with unintelligible Greek whispers. She was at a loss for words and "thank you" was all she could mutter, when without warning, everyone surrounding her was pushed aside like falling trees at the wake of a charging rhino.

A tall woman with the face of a hawk emerged from the crowd and stood before Zoe. She looked to be in her early seventies. Her hawk stare burnt Zoe to the core. Never had an older woman's eyes weighed so deeply upon Zoe. Not her grandma's, nor her mom's. The older woman then cracked a smile and Zoe was uncomfortable once more. It felt as if she was being probed for some unknown reason.

"I am Sophia," said the woman in a thick Greek

accent. She opened her mouth to add something more, but she didn't get the chance.

Another woman of a similar age, shorter in stature but with a much sunnier disposition, sprang behind Sophia and flung herself onto Zoe. Sophia didn't take the interruption lightly, as her flat and silky eyebrows joined in a very disapproving frown. She was now full on looking the part of a hawk.

"Koukla mou! (*My doll!*)" screeched the short woman at Zoe. "Me, Rita!" Her English was elementary at best, but intelligible at heart. "Look, Sophia, she look like Maria!"

"Yes, she is very beautiful," Sophia admitted, as if the words were being dragged out of her.

"We have so much to talk," Rita insisted. "You tells us everytin' about Maria life in America. We three best friends. Maria, Sophia, and me... from little girls, you know," she gestured by placing her hand waist-height to indicate the size of a toddler.

Zoe felt a hundred questions about her grandmother struggling to come out. She just knew these two women were the guardians of Maria's secrets. Odd thing, though. She had a momentary flashback of Maria's last moment at the hospital, a dying ninety-plus old woman. As sick as her grandmother was, she was a woman that looked her age. But Sophia and Rita looked twenty to thirty years younger.

Zoe's train of thought was interrupted by a brief glimpse of her young hero in the crowd. He was standing next to a horse-drawn carriage that had been backed up to the pier. Six elderly men loaded the coffin on it. The young man turned and looked at Zoe. He examined her long and hard, forgetting his very existence. Just then, the horses trotted away, launching the wheeled buggy forward.

"This way," commanded Father Michael, as they

followed the carriage on the cobblestone road. The islanders silently tailed them in a rather disciplined fashion.

Behind them, now free of the dock, the small navy boat revved its motor and backed away from the pier with all navy personnel onboard. It was soon making distance, carrying them and Mr. Kanakis back to Andoriani. He turned to look at Zoe one last time with a disturbed look in his face. She took notice, humphed a touch, then quickly turned her attention back to the procession.

Zoe found herself immersed in a world that time had forgotten. The picturesque fishing boats, the beauty of the scenic village, and the amphitheater series of row houses, left her genuinely speechless. "Gorgeous," was her word of choice, murmuring it to herself repeatedly. The two and three-storied neoclassical mansions with whitewashed, blue and ochre-colored fronts, lilac and cherry-painted doors and shutters, featured traditional wooden and iron balconies decorated by vines and flowerpots with the occasional motley crew of local cats. The never-ending rows of colorful houses were interrupted occasionally by tall fig trees that cast shadows on the winding cobblestone alleys. The village was eerily quiet.

The horse carriage wheels raised a racket in the eerie silence that marked the march. The rustle of the fig tree leaves and the villagers' footsteps echoed louder than their whispers. Zoe felt surprisingly at home in this foreign place. She was being rewarded for her long journey and was able to finally breathe again after the whirlwind of the past two days.

"You don't have cars here?" she let slip to the priest, who was walking by her side.

"Motor cars are prohibited on the island," he replied. "Is it not like your grandmother described?"

"As a matter of fact, Yiayia didn't say much about Petra," she exhaled.

"Oh," replied Father Michael without adding a comment.

Zoe wouldn't know how to explain it even if he asked a thousand questions. She gave the scenery another look, lusciously taking it all in. Her eyes burned brightly from the sun's reflection, bouncing off the colorful houses and the crystal blue sea. She squinted, looked up and about. There were just a few villagers here and there, staring at the procession from a window or a balcony. It was as if the entire island was out there, marching along.

Zoe turned her head back to look at those who were following from behind. Despite their old age, everyone seemed to keep pace with the galloping carriage. She then remembered all that she had read about the place being a Blue Zone. The people looked healthy indeed, and in top form. Zoe noticed Sophia and Rita walking together, the two women fixing their eyes on her. Rita was beaming like a giddy little girl. It was easy to imagine her with a pink bow in her hair, playing hopscotch on chalk drawn squares. Sophia, on the other hand, held to her predatory look despite her painstaking effort to put on a smile.

Zoe felt a shiver up her spine, not knowing what to make of the woman. As a distraction, she glimpsed over to her tall hero who walked next to the carriage. "Wow. What a tall drink of water", she mumbled to herself. He too stole glances in her direction, but as soon as their sights crossed, he averted his gaze elsewhere. Zoe turned to Father Michael, trying her best casual voice.

"Is that man a priest?"

"He is a priest-in-training. And he will be ordained soon," answered the Father, smiling. "He is my son... Paris."

She masked her disappointment as best she could, but couldn't avoid biting her lower lip. "Focus Zoe," she said to herself, looking at Maria's coffin. *You've been secretive your whole life, Yiayia,* she thought. *Suddenly you're speaking volumes. But what are you trying to tell me? Why have you brought me here?*

For no reason, as if she heard an answer, Zoe looked up a hill to her left. An elderly man stood on the highest ground under the shade of a tree, looking down on them. His features were obscured under his white hat that complemented the rest of his sharp, white costume. Zoe could make out a slick, trimmed white beard. But most striking was the red carnation on the man's jacket breast pocket. His wardrobe selection was quite the antithesis to all the islanders' black garments. No one else in the procession seemed to notice the man in white.

"We're almost there," announced the priest.

Zoe looked at her watch, the only dear present she had received from her Yiayia, and she realized that it had stopped. She tapped it lightly, shook it a little.

The villa greeted them at the bend of the road, mottled by vines and surrounded by lush fig trees. It carried an aura of abandonment, with sad, wind-beaten shutters that hung lopsided. It was a neo-classical two-story villa just outside of town, the kind of home people with royal character used to build in the past. The architecture respected the lineage of houses that celebrated the Aegean islands. Although this one was a touch more opulent than the facades Zoe had just seen in the village. Patches of plaster were missing from its once white walls.

"This was your grandmother's home. And it now

belongs to you," declared Father Michael, stepping closer to the door.

"For seventy years, no one step foot here," added Rita, in her broken English, penetrating Zoe with her eyes. As if her words carried a special meaning.

Zoe was beyond speechless. Her ownership of this property was surprising news to her. Father Michael clutched the door, pushing it open.

"There are no locks on the island," he revealed with a grin, then stepped aside from her. "We have nothing to hide."

Zoe sauntered in not knowing what to think. All she knew was that Yiayia had refused to speak of her past life in Greece, and Zoe desperately wanted to get to the bottom of it. Instead, she was greeted by darkness, gobs of dust, and cobwebs that climbed up to the ceiling covering its ornate chandeliers and decorative crown molding. The once lavish wallpaper was peeling off the walls, revealing discolored patches from missing pictures frames. Drop sheets covered the furniture in the stateroom, and mysterious antiques filled every other nook and cranny.

"The ghosts of Grandma's secrets..." thought Zoe, marveling and smirking.

The air was stifling. The place tasted like mothballs and the room temperature was unbearably hot. Sensing her discomfort, Sophia and Rita swooped right into the villa and pushed open the shutters, which instantly let the sunshine and fresh air in. The ladies continued their hurried housework by removing drop sheets from the furniture, revealing a well-appointed room. They quickly folded the linens, then stored them away.

Zoe approached the windows and glanced outside. Her view was of the glorious harbor below, seen descending between red-tiled rooftops and verandas overflowing with flowers. Before she could react to any of it, Paris and the pallbearers carried the silver coffin into the salon, gently resting it on a 19th century Victorian dining table in the middle of the room. Zoe looked at Father Michael perplexed.

"I thought we were going to the church?" she asked.

"The funeral is tomorrow," said the priest. "Tonight we shall keep wake for Maria."

"It's tradition," added Sophia, looking coldly at Zoe.

"All right, then…" was all she had time to say.

The procession of mourners began entering the house to view the coffin, mumbling prayers in Greek. One of them propped a holy icon on the table.

"Saint Peter," explained Father Michael. "He's the Patron Saint of the island."

Rita cut right through the crowd and reached for the coffin's lid. She grasped its edges and began to pull.

"What are you fixing to do?" yelled Sophia in Greek, rushing to stop her.

"I want to see my friend!" bellowed Rita in Greek, with the innocence of a child.

Zoe was rendered speechless at the spectacle of the two women struggling right over her grandma's coffin. Some people shouted in Greek, but none dared to physically intervene.

"No!" yelled Sophia. "She's been dead for days. Her remains have undoubtedly—"

But it was too late to stop Rita's determination. She popped the lid open to a chorus of shocked reactions.

Zoe cupped her mouth to avoid shrieking. She launched herself toward the coffin in an attempt to shut it just as the whole room behind her held its bated breath. And there she was… her Grandma Maria for all to see. But she was glowing with a hint of a smile, as if she was taking a nap, her hands clasped against her chest in prayer. Rita reached in for a full-body sniff.

"She smells like jasmine, haaa!" she uttered almost triumphantly.

Zoe was shocked. Her grandmother looked much younger than she remembered. This was not the woman who died in her arms just a few days ago! The mourners all made the sign of the cross and sighed. Sophia grabbed Rita by the arm and whisked her away.

"We must take care of our guests. Come now!" she insisted.

"But I want to be with Maria. I've missed her," protested Rita, feeble under Sophia's spell. The hawkish woman extended her hand to Zoe, too.

"Join us in the kitchen. We must prepare for the wake."

Zoe had absolutely no idea what to do, no idea what was expected of her. All these funeral customs, were well... all Greek to her.

"Don't worry. We'll help you," added Sophia, tugging her along.

She ushered Zoe into the hall that led to the kitchen, but not before Zoe took one last look into the living room and saw Paris leaning over the coffin, staring solemnly at her grandmother, his eyes welling up.

The kitchen was narrow with tall cupboards, marble countertops, a stove and an equal amount of dust. The older ladies swung open the windows, desperate for some air. The sun's rays burst like laser beams through the leaves of a big, old fig tree. Elderly ladies flooded into the confined space carrying baked goods, other provisions, and coffee pots. The sink's faucet raised quite the racket before finally releasing water. It was then left to run, allowing the century aged pipes to self-clean. Dozens of old lady hands went to work, brushing the kitchen clean, lighting kindle wood to warm the stove, filling plates with biscotti, pouring brandy in cups and boiling boundless pots of coffee. Zoe looked out of her element.

"How can I help?" she asked.

Zoe felt awkward, very much like an American tourist than an archetypal Greek woman. Back home—in Queens —she was the queen of her castle, and she sure knew how to entertain and took great pride in it. But here she was out of her league and felt less of a lady. As if reading her mind, Rita approached Zoe and took her hand in a comforting fashion.

"Sooo? How long you stay?" asked the short woman, all smiles.

That was a good question indeed. For just a few minutes ago, Zoe was unaware that she was the owner of a fabulous villa.

"A couple of days," she answered, as that was her initial plan and the honest-to-god truth. "I have a business back home and I must get back soon," she added, her mind racing. "But now that Grandma has left me this big old house, well, I may stay a little longer! You know, to try and sell it...?"

Zoe scrutinized the cracked kitchen walls as she talked. But when she lowered her eyes again, she realized all the ladies were staring at her, the sounds of hissing and steaming coffee pots all but ignored. An earthquake could have rumbled through the middle of the kitchen and they would have ignored that too. Zoe looked caught in the headlights. Someone had to break the silence. But none of the elderly ladies dared to speak up, except for Sophia.

"There is no real estate value here," Sophia remarked in a dry tone, very much in control.

"But we're in Greece! One of the world's top destinations... You can't scroll through Facebook nor Instagram without seeing photos of followers island-hopping from Mykonos to Santorini to—" Zoe shot back, smirking and rolling her eyes. The old ladies shrugged their shoulders at the words "Facebook", "Instagram" and "followers", having no clue what any of that meant.

"Petra is difficult to access for tourists. We're unlike the other, bigger islands."

Zoe felt a pang of disappointment. But that didn't stop her brain from working.

"I know! We'll bring onboard an international realtor—like Sotheby's or Christie's—you know, put it on the real market, see what it fetches."

"You need not agonize, my dear. We shall take care of everything for you. Perhaps find you a local buyer, here, on Petra?"

"That could work, I guess..." Zoe was now physically tired and looking defeated.

The old ladies let out a long, communal breath. Sophia greeted her with a cold smile.

"Good. We will handle all the paperwork, not to worry..." she added. "But today is a celebration. We are returning our best friend to her origins, where she belongs."

Sophia grabbed a glass, filled it with brandy and handed it to Zoe. She then passed another to Rita and raised one herself.

"To Maria!"

The rest of the women raised their glasses.

"To Yiayia!" added Zoe.

"Ya Mas! (*Cheers!*)" cheered Rita, as everybody downed the brandy.

Zoe was no stranger to alcohol having been a party girl in her days, but this brew proved a bit too exotic for her throat. She grimaced, eliciting a good-natured laugh at her expense. All the ladies grinned wholeheartedly at Zoe, except for Sophia, who was way too busy in her head.

Zoe made the rounds of the house carrying a silver tray chock-full of steaming coffee cups and glasses of brandy. She offered the drinks to the mourners who gave their condolences in return. Copious baskets of big, juicy figs were placed on the table beside the coffin.

Father Michael informed her that the fig is an important fruit on the island and is commonly offered to the deceased for the afterlife. There was a lot for Zoe to process, and she was simply exhausted. Her jet lag was really taking its toll. Her knees were buckling and her eyelids felt heavy. Every wink was paralyzing. She was seeing double and the serving tray shook wildly in her hands. She watched in slow motion as the remaining cups on the tray started sliding down onto one side and there was nothing she could do about it. Just then, Paris reached in and steadied his hand under hers. They locked eyes and she instantly blushed again.

"I got it," she said.

"Are you sure?"

He sounded concerned. Zoe was certain he was not flirting.

"Yes. Thank you."

He let her go and nicked a glass of brandy for himself.

"May you live long and remember her," he added.

"Thank you," she repeated, wishing she had something clever to say. She nodded, cracked a tiny smile, and timidly walked away. Rita was waiting for her by the kitchen door.

"Sooo... whaaa you think?" Rita beamed. "He handsome devil, no?"

They looked at each other, Zoe wondering if Rita could actually read her mind. Rita giggled like a conspiring teenager.

"Before he takes his vows, he will marry Eleni. My granddaughter," interjected Sophia, eyeballing them both. "It has been arranged."

Rita sprang before Zoe could react.

"Nahhh. You crazy," she shot back at Sophia with the best English she could muster. "Paris no want fix marriage."

And as if to add insult to injury, Rita turned to Zoe. "Sooo, you have boyfriend?"

"Haaa! It's true what they say. You Greeks really work fast," replied Zoe, laughing.

"When is 'bout love, yes!" answered Rita, joining her in laughter. "No waste the time, you know... Paris, he must marry before he takes vows, or he no marry after."

"He sounds complicated," cracked Zoe. "I don't know if my schedule permits."

Rita grasped Zoe's hands tightly, with a spark of alarm in her voice.

"You must make the time, my dear. Before you know, you will be old hag like me. Bahaha! And me, I give up eternal life to be in love again..."

"Cease this senseless babble and hop to it!" barked Sophia. "We have guests waiting on us."

Zoe ignored the outburst.

"Did you two really grow up with my grandmother?"

"We were... how you say... *in-separable*," shined Rita.

"Yiayia was almost ninety-seven years old when she died. I mean, you both look decades younger..."

Sophia laughed hysterically, but Zoe noticed how ill at ease Rita appeared to be.

"It is our Mediterranean diet, of course," bragged Sophia. "Petra has the healthiest climate."

Zoe turned to Rita, waiting for a rebuttal. Instead,

Sophia thrust a full tray of biscotti into the short woman's hands, scolding her with a venomous stare.

"I'm so sorry. I say too much, you know... Is the brandy," muttered Rita, avoiding Zoe's eyes.

She then exited the kitchen with the tray of cookies, leaving Sophia and Zoe behind. The two women turned away from each other, busying themselves in their serving duties.

The relentless chatter rumbling from the living room seized abruptly. The sudden silence was so deafening, it was felt all the way into the kitchen. Zoe, shadowed by the rest of the women, filed into the salon to see what the fuss was all about.

She recognized the man with the white suit and hat. He stood at the door, his eyes fixed on the open coffin. All those gathered gawked at him, speechless. They reacted with mixed feelings; from a hint of awe, to utter disdain. Zoe was struck by Sophia's look, an undisguised hot hatred that radiated from the hawk woman's eyes. The man in white commanded a distinguishing presence. He did not look like the rest of the islanders. Zoe did not remember ever seeing eyes that blue before in her life. Paris' eyes came a close second.

The stranger's bone structure could have been described as Nordic. His skin was pinkish and his silver hair and thick goatee were well-groomed. He removed his hat and respectfully approached the casket. As he hovered over Maria's remains, the image looked like a Caravaggio painting. He reached in with his free hand and brushed the tips of his fingers over her cheek. Zoe saw him mouth one word; her grandmother's name. At first, it looked as if he was bowing to Maria, but Zoe's eyes widened as she saw the mysterious man give her grandma a lingering, sweet kiss on the lips. She

21

looked around the room to make sure she wasn't the only one seeing this. By this point, most of the mourners had turned their eyes down, studying the cracks on the ceramic floor.

Zoe looked about to burst. She wanted to know who this man was! Just as she was about to say something, she caught a glimpse of Rita looking alarmed. She waved to Zoe with her hand, motioning her not to interfere. Sophia had her eyes fixed on the floor too, with her hands scrunched into fists. The man put on his hat, removed the red carnation from his chest and placed it in Maria's hands. He then turned to look at Zoe, gave her a nod, pivoted and split, his every step and manner a motion of elegance. The very moment he was out of sight, the incessant chatter in the villa returned. Father Michael came to her side.

"Who was that man?" she asked before the priest could say a word.

"Stefanos, an island character..." he explained awkwardly, unsure how to continue.

"He seemed to know my grandmother well."

"Well, he did..." Father Michael paused.

Zoe sensed his embarrassment. She suddenly felt unwell, as if she was about to faint.

"I am sorry, Father," she said. "I'm exhausted. Jet lag, and all..."

"Of course, forgive us. We have overwhelmed you. You need to rest... We will tend to the wake."

Zoe hadn't realized that Sophia had approached them until the tall woman spoke.

"There is a bedroom upstairs. Let me take you..."

"Thank you. I'll find it myself," she muttered with as much resistance as she could muster. Zoe let out a great breath and turned to face the stairs. She ambled over, grabbing hold of the banister for support and sluggishly took the steps up to the villa's second floor, brushing the blur of the lively living room away.

She followed a long hallway, lined with more peeling walls and discolored patches from missing picture frames. The master bedroom was behind the first door she tried. The shutters outside the windows were wide open, giving view to a bright red sunset. She pulled the drop sheet from the bed and she laid heavy on its thick mattress. Was any of this real? Maybe she was still asleep in her New York City flat? A villa of her own, what a thought! Innumerable questions laid thick, weighing her head down on the soft pillow. But for now, she badly needed to sleep. She managed just enough energy to kick her boots off, and that was all she could remove. She gazed at a leaky rain mark on the ceiling before her heavy eyelids obscured it. She dreamt Yiayia Maria was here with her and Zoe was once again a little girl. "Am I a *real* Greek, Grandma?"

Her grandmother was a thing of beauty. The wrinkles of time could not obscure the truth. She was elegant in her fashion sense and in her character. Her visits with Zoe were brief, but she cast a deep impression on her granddaughter. Maria had been the inspiration behind "Zoe's Blue Jeans Shoppe" in Queens. "I'm trying my best, Grandma," she said, seeing tears in Maria's eyes. She had never noticed such sadness in her grandmother's face before. Maria hugged her infant granddaughter tight, sobbing. "Ekaterini mou (*My Ekaterini*)," she said. "I'm Zoe," replied the little girl, all confused.

At that very moment, sleep just overtook Zoe. "Who is *Ekaterini...*?" was her last conscious thought.

TWO
FIG TREE

1944

A noise woke her up. Maria shot up to her feet, breathless. She had fallen asleep on the armchair in the living room. It was still black out and the night was decisively quiet. The gunfire and the distant explosions had seized. Peace at last, she thought. The nightmare was over. The Germans were running. The Greek partisans were doggedly sticking to the Nazi tail, making them pay dearly for their brutal crimes.

Maria dragged her feet to the window and looked out. All the lights down in the village were on. No one was sleeping tonight. She could taste the dawn of freedom. But what was the noise that woke her up? She shook the sleep off her, rolled her head from side to side. The last couple of days were rough. She was running aid up to the resistance fighters hiding in the hills, carrying ammunition and other supplies. Sophia was there, too, a fury on a warpath. Maria sensed the vengeance burning in her friend's eyes. Sophia wanted Nazi heads to roll in retribution for her dead father and brothers. But today Maria had seen enough killing and eventually found her way back home. The occupation of Greece was officially over, and so, she decided to sit and wait for peace... at least wait for dawn.

It was a thud on the door that broke her sleep. Maria had been weary of knock-knocks during the entire occupation. In fact, there were no few instances of German boots kicking down her door in search of partisans or for any reason they deemed appropriate. But this time, she gingerly approached the front door and laid her palm on its surface to listen in. Silence. She didn't hear a peep, nothing suspicious shuffling outside. She pulled on the handle and swung the door open violently ready for any surprise. Maria wasn't afraid. And instead of a sneak attack, she was met with nothing but stillness. And peace. And quiet. She must have simply dreamt the clamor on the door. She shook her head, giggled ever so lightly, and just as she was about to step back in she noticed a pool of blood on the doorstep that led to the dark bushes in her garden.

Without thinking, Maria turned back into the hall table and grabbed a lantern that was burning something fierce. She charged fearlessly down the front steps, raising a bright light over her garden, and coolly glided barefoot on the rocks.

"Is anyone there?" she asked.

That's when she saw him. The man was lying on the flowerbed turned to his side, feebly crawling. She immediately ran to his side. Maria was sure he was a wounded partisan looking for a helping hand. But what was he doing here? Her aunt's villa was out of the way, hidden from the rest of the village. And why was he alone? Who was he? Maria took pride in knowing all the resistance fighters in Petra, even some who had snuck over from the main island. She kneeled and turned him onto his back.

"Who are you? What happened?" she asked.

Her hands were now entirely drenched in his blood. She raised her lantern to get a better look of him. He was smeared red and riddled with holes, like a chunk of Swiss cheese. His face was lacerated and unrecognizable.

"I'll take you inside where I can help you. Can you walk?" she asked, but all she heard were moans. He could barely breathe, let alone utter a word.

Just as she was about to lift him, something caught her eye. Her lantern revealed the undeniable pattern of a Nazi uniform. Without an iota of conscious thought, she dropped him and tore into the kitchen, snatching the biggest knife she could find and dashed back out, animal instinct coursing through her veins. She had a mortal enemy exactly right where she wanted him. And she was going to finish him, even if he was running for his life. In Maria's mind, he was not human. So she aimed for his throat. And a one, and a two, and a... That's when the man started coughing violently and spitting out blood. He was an awful sight to see. At that very moment, Maria was flushed with a jolt of empathy. She lowered her knife a touch, still keeping it close to his bloodied face.

"Why did you come here?" she griped, looking for answers. She was suddenly very afraid; afraid that she was not making the right decision, afraid that she was not thinking straight. Her heart raced, galloped, contorted. Her mind rushed back to when she was a kid and how she nursed foxes and snakes and all kinds of dangerous creatures back to life. Maria paused to think for a moment, took in one long deep breath, then exhaled. She dropped the knife and with all the strength she could muster, she snatched the wounded German soldier by his feet and dragged him into her opulent villa.

She dropped him on the stateroom floor and cautiously closed the front door, hoping no one had seen her. Her heart beat fast. She may have shut the island out for the time being, but in here, she had to face down her own ancestors. They all stared at Maria from their framed positions on the walls. She had lost her father and uncles to the Italians in the War of Albania. Her aunt, the woman who had raised her from a little child, had passed away during the German occupation, stricken by pneumonia. Serious, hard, unforgiving eyes, Maria was being judged by all the ghosts in the picture frames. And she knew it was only going to get worse. As she lit a candle next to the man, she let out a frightening scream. She recognized him! He was not a mere foot soldier. It was Captain Stephan Mueller, the one in charge of the excavation at Shepherd's Highland!

Maria covered her eyes and relived the mass execution. Thirty-three men from Petra were executed for the killing of one German soldier. It was, of course, at the order of the Nazi Colonel who turned up from Andoriani with blood in his eyes. It was the Colonel who had shouted "FIRE". Maria remembered Captain Mueller averting his eyes from the massacre. It had made an impression on her.

"Why my home, of all places?" she shouted.

Maria laid him on a blue and narrow Persian rug and dragged him all the way to the kitchen. She ripped his uniform open and washed his body with raki; an unsweetened, anise-flavored alcoholic drink popular in the Greek Islands. She gulped some raki to take off the edge, and even poured a few ounces down his throat for good measure. She examined his naked torso and noticed two bullet holes and dozens of stab wounds. She ignored his shrieks of pain as she removed the shells and stitched his cuts. Maria was cool, calm, collected. She had been to this rodeo before. She ripped bed sheets into ribbons and used them to dress his injuries. By the time she was done, Captain Stephan Mueller was out cold.

The soft light of dawn began to paint the windows golden as she prayed in the kitchen under its glow. She hoped for this day to pass uneventfully. Maria placed a blanket on him as he slept, and she left the house to join the clamorous celebration down at the harbor. The bay was chock-full of fishing boats proudly sporting the regal blue and white colors of the Greek flag. Maria beamed and waved at everyone, making sure to play the part in order to avoid any suspicion. If word got out that she was hiding the enemy in her home, she, along with her uninvited house-guest would be goners. But she was a keen one, her aunt having taught her everything she knew. No one could pull the wool over Maria's eyes, oh no. Throughout the years, many single fishermen tried to cast their nets on her, but she wouldn't have any of it. She was the catch that always got away. She was way too smart for Petra, even if she barely finished grade school. She knew it. And everyone in this small cluster of islands knew it. They were all expecting her to leave the island one day, but not today. Today she had a new mission: to save an enemy soldier and to show the rest of the world just how loving and compassionate the Modern Greeks—who suffered for the last five centuries at the hands of oppressors—can be. So she recruited two very special allies for this quest. Rita and Dimitri helped her carry the Captain upstairs to the master bedroom. They too had their fair share of pain from the war, but they were the kindest souls Maria ever knew.

"I'm doing this for you, not him," Rita cried to her.

She knew the secret would be safe with them for a

while. Captain Mueller's sojourn in Petra was unblemished until the reprisals. He had shown great sympathy for the locals from the very start of his arrival on Petra. His small troop of men stationed at Shepherd's Highland at the north end of the island, got busy digging the site for clandestine reasons. They kept out of the islanders' sights, always making sure to stay out of their way. But that fragile trust was all but destroyed the day he handpicked the local men to be shot. Though most of the islanders knew his hand was forced by the higher Wehrmacht command on Andoriani. Still, there was no way they could ever forgive him.

She did what she could with the man's wounds. Her deceased aunt Erato had taught her well on the secrets of the plants. Maria still kept several miracle potions in her cupboard made with magical ingredients only found in Petra's flora. She would always say that her aunt was one of those women that had been "touched by the stars". Erato had created wondrous medicines made out of flowers, roots and fruits. She even made yummy jams and teas on the side. Erato also had the uncanny ability to see the future inside an empty coffee cup, to foretell the weather from the path of flying birds, and also to ward off the evil eye. When Maria lost her aunt two winters ago, she survived mostly with those learnt skills. For some bread, butter or just a couple of eggs, she helped the locals by providing ointments against warts, bad luck or even lovesickness.

She cleaned Mueller's wounds several times a day with ointments, applied some miracle paste, and changed his bandages. The rest was up to the gods. There was no telling how much blood the man had lost. His body would have to replenish itself on its own. And so, some rough nights followed. Stricken by nightmares, the German screamed and tossed about. Maria held vigil for him, holding him down and tending to his stitches, always praying that none of the villagers would hear his painful screams.

Then one morning, she entered the master bedroom and found his eyes open, staring at the window. Captain Mueller saw her but gave no indications that he knew her, nor that he understood exactly where he was.

"Dead?…" he mumbled.

"No, you're not dead," she berated him. "But you should be. You're a murderer. Do you understand? A murderer!"

"Nero," he groaned in Greek, meaning *water*.

He was incapable of tending to himself in any capacity. Maria helped him drink, fed him and changed his sheets as needed with the help of Dimitri. She didn't sleep well most nights, constantly worried that she would be discovered. Yet to her dismay, that was not all she worried about.

She would hear the echo of distant thunder, but kept dismissing it until one day she tried something for the very first time. She brewed herself a cup of coffee and sat in the stateroom like she had done so many times before with her aunt. Erato always enjoyed a cigarette with her coffee, but Maria never touched tobacco. "It helps with the magic… and it helps me breathe," her aunt would always say, while elegantly blowing smoke. Maria was taught to watch the shapes that formed inside the swirling smoke while trying to see angels and demons whispering the secrets of things to come.

With her last sip, Maria overturned the cup on its saucer and waited a few minutes. With fingers trembling, she turned the cup again and looked inside. There it was on the smeared porcelain, the whole truth for her to see. Aunt Erato had taught her well, and there was no mistaking the will of the gods. It did not cheer her up, knowing this newfound truth. She knew only time would tell if it became reality. She shook her head in disgust and pushed the coffee cup away.

~

By the third week, Captain Mueller managed to sit up on his own. Maria plopped a bowl of figs on his lap to eat. He was barely beginning to regain his primary functions. He fumbled with the fruit, managing to feed himself somehow while smearing his chin with nectar juice.

"You eat like a baby," she goaded him, drawing a chair by his bedside. She sat and skinned the figs for him.

He pointed to the tree outside the window.

"Your figs?"

"Yes, from my tree. My aunt planted it when she was a little girl. Petra has many fig trees. Thank God you Germans didn't strip them bare like everything else. We had to feed ourselves somehow," she snarled, pushing a fig into his mouth.

He chewed and swallowed it with great effort, never taking his eyes off her.

"I never meant for you people to suffer..." he pleaded in Greek. Maria remembered he had demonstrated his knowledge of Greek in the past, trying to get on the islanders' good side. "I am a geology professor. I teach... I'm not a murderer. I like gardening—it's my hobby. I love growing things, caring for them... Do you have flowers in your garden?"

"Some," she muttered, feeling bothered by the small talk.

"What kind?"

"I have garifallies (*carnations*)," she answered.

He looked puzzled. She ignored him and got up. She felt being drawn into a conversation with this man and resented herself for it. Just as she turned to leave—

"Could you please open the window?" he pleaded. She sighed and slid it open for him. "I like hearing the wind, the birds. Sometimes I can almost hear the sea..."

She marched out without saying a word. A slight sea breeze rustled the fig leaves.

Stephan Mueller, the man, was alive and thankful. He tried to adjust himself on the pillow but winced in pain. He rested his head back and closed his eyes, falling asleep.

When he woke up, there was a vase filled with carnations at the end table by his side.

THREE
REPAST

The morning light bathed the master bedroom, gently removing the sleep out of her eyes. Zoe heard the cries of seagulls from a distance, soothing her senses. She felt refreshed and stretched out in delight. But the feeling didn't last long. She noticed Sophia sitting there on a chair, observing her. The hawk woman's lips formed a smile, though there was no cheer in her penetrating eyes. Startled, Zoe's first thought was asking her how long she'd been there but decided against it.

"What time is it?" she asked instead.

Sophia showed her empty wrists, wiggling her head.

"I don't have a watch. The sun is quite high now, that's all I know... Sleep well?"

"Yes, very restful," commented Zoe as she fumbled for her wristwatch on the end table. The watch had stopped again despite the fact that she wound it last night. She reached for her smartphone and found it equally dead.

"I don't suppose you have cell service on the island?" Zoe inquired. Sophia shook her head.

"Up up. Time to take Maria to church," Sophia said.

She then got up and walked to the door. "I will put you in touch with the notary after... to sell the house, yes?"

Zoe turned and set her feet on the floor. She twirled her toes to wake them up.

"Wait. What do you think I could get for it?"

"Too soon to talk about money now. Later," emphasized Sophia as she stepped out.

Zoe explored the upper floor until she located the bathroom. Thankfully, it had a tub and a fixed shower head. Her on the go New York-ness kicked in and she flung her clothes off fast. The pipes protested, but they eventually released clean water. It was a good call on her part to have picked up a bottle of shampoo at the JFK Duty Free. The water was cold and an excellent picker-upper. Ready to face a new day, she hunted through her luggage for a black shirt and skirt that she had brought for the occasion.

The entire island was at the villa's doorstep patiently waiting for her. Amid the many solemn faces, Rita's was the beam of sunshine that lifted Zoe's spirit.

"Is time to lay Maria for rest," said the petite woman with her unique cheery disposition and charming enunciation.

Six elderly men in their Sunday best waited to carry the casket to the church. They anticipated her signal.

"I need a moment alone with Yiayia," she pled and Rita nodded.

Zoe entered the villa and approached the table at the center of the stateroom, baskets of figs enveloping the casket. She was still amazed at the sight of the dead woman's beauty. She reached for her grandma's silver mane and felt its silky touch as she brushed it with her fingers.

"Truth be told, you really do look amazing, Yiayia. I guess this island does agree with you," as Zoe looked around the elegant home. "Is this what you've been hiding from me all these years, or is there more?"

She planted a sweet kiss on her grandma's forehead. "I hope you're finally at peace. I love you."

Zoe exited and joined the procession as the pallbearers carried the silver coffin out of the villa. Father Michael, Sophia and Rita rounded off the head of the pack on the way to church.

According to Google, Petra's Saint Peter's Church was erected on the foundation of an ancient Greek temple devoted to Aphrodite—the goddess of love. During the Ottoman occupation, a young Petrian girl claimed to have seen Saint Peter in her dream, directing her to the site of the ruins. There, an old Byzantine painting of the apostle was unearthed. And just as the dream had instructed, the islanders built a Christian Orthodox church on that very spot. The church was set ablaze by the Ottomans, and a second time by the Venetians centuries later. Many Byzantine artworks didn't survive, but the inner sanctum still featured a marble sculpture with the likeness of the goddess of love. The church was modest, but incredibly pretty. Jarring, rotted-out scaffoldings surrounded the bell clock tower, as if renovations had been abandoned decades ago. Zoe noticed plaster patches on the broken mortar that scarred the tower with its great clock almost pushed out of its socket. Time had stopped in its dials just minutes before twelve. Next to the tower, and looking completely out of place, was a small tool shack.

Inside, the church was overrun to the rafters with townspeople, hundreds of candles burning everywhere. Old ladies fanned their sweaty faces. It was stifling hot and suffocating. Even the churchgoers looked about ready to melt. Everybody made way for Zoe as she walked up to the front pew and took a seat next to her grandmother's casket. She was pleased to see Paris next to Father Michael in the inner sanctum. Cloaked with priest-like garments, he assisted his father in the funeral service. At one point, Paris looked at her and she smiled. Was this appropriate, she asked herself, while lowering her eyes regretfully?

"I can't understand you, Zoe. Why don't you wanna travel to Greece? How I'd love to go and find myself a Greek shepherd boy with a hairy chest and big hands who can make the hills tremble under our passion." *Good going Zoe, perfect time to recall your friend Patricia's deviant fantasies, she thought to herself.* "A priest is a kind of shepherd, isn't he?" Patricia now mysteriously whispering in her ear, making Zoe bite her lower lip to prevent any unexpected giggles.

She quickly changed her train of thought by remembering the man in white from yesterday, the one named Stefanos. She scanned the congregation in search of him, but he wasn't around. Paris and Father Michael locked stares, with the priest nodding to his son with a go-ahead. Paris stepped forward towards the congregation and looked solemnly at the open casket as he chanted.

"*Have mercy on us, o God, according to your great mercy; listen, and have mercy. Again we pray for the repose of the soul of the servant of God, Maria Artemisou, departed this life; and for the forgiveness of her every transgression, voluntary; and involuntary. Let the Lord establish her soul where the Just repose; the mercies of God, the Kingdom of the Heavens, and the remission of her sins; let us ask of Christ our immortal King, and our God. Let us pray to the Lord."*

If there was ever a moment, this was the one where Zoe felt utterly smitten. She noticed Father Michael behind his son, wiping a tear. It was indeed an impeccable delivery.

~

The cemetery was just behind the church. Maria's coffin was lowered into the ground at a patch marked by graves that looked freshly groomed. The rest of the plots in the graveyard were overwhelmed by weeds, bushes and other wild growths. Old tombstones and broken crosses hid behind thick foliage. Father Michael sprinkled the coffin with holy oil as the bearers approached the grave.

"You shall sprinkle me with hyssop and I shall be clean. You shall wash me and I shall be whiter than snow."

Paris helped the men lower Maria's casket into the ground. The mourners all took turns tossing handfuls of earth on the casket.

"The earth is the Lord's, and the fullness thereof; the world, and all that dwell therein. You are dust, and to dust you will return."

Kostas, the diminutive 80-year-old local carpenter and cemetery caretaker, began emptying the back-fill soil into the grave. He looked worn out, disorganized, and reluctant. All in attendance noticed he was completely out of place except for Zoe, who was consumed with tears filling her eyes. It was a great release. Zoe thought it odd that not one tear was shed the moment Yiayia died in her hands just days ago. She thought she had too much New York in her. But here, "I'm indeed a *real* Greek Yiayia," she mumbled to herself. As she wiped her eyes, her gaze fell on a neighboring tombstone. *Georgios Sotiriou, February 1847 – August 2015.*

"This can't be right," she thought, but then something else quickly caught her attention. Stefanos was watching the funeral from the other end of the cemetery, standing behind the rusted ruins of an older gate. Zoe excused herself and pushed through the weeds to reach him. He saw her coming, so he turned around and left, skipping through a narrow path. She was so irritated by the man's behavior. "You can't run forever," she mumbled to herself.

The repast was staged in the town square right next to the church. The townspeople had arranged the tables from the only tavern in the plaza. It was a festive array of colorful plaid tablecloths covered with a massive post-funeral feast. The tavern belonged to Nikos; he was introduced to Zoe as Sophia's husband. He was the typical "OPA!" type Greek, the kind Hollywood easily satirized, she thought. He was a pleasant enough fellow, making Zoe question his choice for a wife. Wine flowed freely and Nikos came to fill her cup.

"Our thoughts are with you, my dear," he charmed. "We wish to make your stay as pleasant as possible."

"Thank you. You're very kind." Zoe grinned from ear to ear.

All those gathered lined up at her table and offered their condolences anew, before taking their seats for the commemoration. She noticed a few new faces. Some had come from distant settlements on the island. In each face, she was introduced to a small piece of the puzzle that made up Yiayia Maria. Zoe listened in on brief anecdotes from her grandma's childhood years. Maria was apparently wild and always in trouble. She was also a loyal friend. She protected the underdog and loved animals. She supported the Greek partisans during the war.

Across the table, Zoe noticed Sophia and Rita sitting together. "Are these two ever apart?" she thought. She so badly wanted to talk to Rita alone, to get some much-needed answers to a hundred questions swarming in her head. With the commiserations over, Zoe found herself face-to-face with Paris. Before she could get up to salute him, he sat right next to her, offering an overflowing plate filled with pastries.

"Homemade custard pie," he indicated. "*Galaktoboureko*. The best in the Dodecanese."

"Oh, thank you…" she answered, genuinely touched.

"You must try it."

He cut a tiny piece, forked it and fed it to her under his blue gaze. She obliged and smiled, nodding in delight. The villagers watched in disbelief, but only Rita craftily beamed.

"Oh wow," Zoe thrilled. "I had Greek galaktoboureko once in a place in Astoria, but this… Did you make it? Your mom?"

Paris produced a bitter smile. He shook his head.

"My father made it. He's famous for his custard pie."

"He's divine…! I'm Zoe, by the way," extending her hand.

"And I'm Paris," shaking her hand.

"Out of the Prince of Troy?"

"Haaa! No. Out of the city, unfortunately. My mother was French."

"Was…?"

"She died when I was a boy."

"Oh, I'm sorry."

He dismissed it with a simple shrug of his shoulders.

"It was a long time ago… Now I've heard lots of stories about your grandma," he added. "She must have been a very… *awesome* lady."

His attempt at American speak was too cute for Zoe not to smile.

"So I hear, too! And I was hoping to learn more from you all..."

"She was well before my time, I'm afraid. Maybe my father could share a story or two."

Zoe was sure the hawk woman was watching. Regardless, she ignored her sixth sense and raised her cup.

"Ya mas!" she cheered.

"Ya mas!" he replied, completing the toast with her.

"Seems like we're the only young people on this whole island," she commented.

"Well yes. They've all left for Andoriani or the mainland. Petra has its charms; the beaches, the blue skies, the food. But not much else."

"If you ask me, this place looks tailor-made for MAMMA MIA!"

He looked at her clueless, totally unaware of her reference. She took another gulp of wine and tried another approach.

"Thank you for the beautiful service earlier. My grandma would have been pleased."

"That was my first funeral service, actually. We don't have many of them around here. Not as far as I can remember..."

"Oh?"

Paris realized her eyes were locked onto his. He casually looked away.

"Anyway. Most days I'm busy tinkering with my clock..."

"Tinkering with your clock?" Zoe looked confused, didn't know how to react.

He motioned towards the bell tower of the church.

"You must have noticed the bell clock over there. As

you can see, it's in need of tinkering. And I'm the only one who cares."

She instinctively looked at her watch.

"It stopped again."

"It's been stopped for a long while. My mission is to have it working again…"

Their chat was interrupted by a sudden commotion at the tavern's entrance. The diners turned to look, but soon returned to eating immediately after acknowledging the two culprits. Nikos was arguing with a man wearing blue jeans. Zoe thought this odd, as everyone else was wearing Mediterranean funeral black. Plus, his short sleeved yellow shirt was unbuttoned, letting loose a sun-roasted belly that hung impressively over his obnoxiously tacky belt buckle. The stranger's eyes were shielded by sunglasses and his head covered with a straw hat. The man was trying to pry a bottle of wine from Nikos' hands.

"That's Aaron," Paris explained to Zoe, as if that meant anything to her.

"Does this happen often?"

"Excuse me," Paris added and left her side.

Zoe watched as the young priest-in-training approached the two men. They stopped their commotion the moment they realized he was approaching. Paris took the unopened bottle of wine from Nikos and gave it to Aaron. Nikos raised his arms in disbelief and re-entered the tavern, followed closely behind by Sophia. Paris then whispered into the Aaron's ear. As Aaron listened, he stole momentary glances at Zoe, nodding his head several times. Then, to Zoe's surprise, he walked toward her. He stopped just as his belly bumped the edge of her table and offered his free hand.

"Excuse me, ma'am," he begged. "I behaved like an oaf during your bereavement meal."

His lips were pudgy and baby-like, as Zoe would later describe them. Wicked sideburns and a three-day beard rounded out his face. She took his hand and shook it, doubly shocked by his US Southern drawl.

"Are you an American?" she asked.

He smiled crookedly.

"I was… in another life."

Sophia came back out of the tavern with her usual stern look and folded arms. She coughed loudly at Aaron. He got the message, but didn't turn to look at her.

"Nice to have met you, ma'am."

Even though Aaron didn't remove his sunglasses, Zoe was sure he winked at her.

"See ya 'round," he said, leaving with the bottle of wine in hand.

She looked down at her smartphone once again in disappointment. No signal and no time. Father Michael approached her with a warm smile.

"Is everything alright?" he asked.

She pointed at the departing Aaron.

"He sure loves his wine."

"That he does," he agreed. "He's such a character."

"There seem to be lots of them in Petra, Father. *Characters.*"

He looked at her, embarrassed, so she changed the subject.

"I need to make a phone call. Is there a public phone around?"

"There's a mini market just a few steps down the road. It says "Manos" out front. You can't miss it," continued Father Michael.

She had left the town square behind when she saw it, with the unmistakable telephone sign protruding from its doorframe. The store was nestled between some pink-colored houses with a cul-de-sac to the left, ending with a cliff overlooking the sea. A man was standing there, his back to her, staring out into the horizon. She was sure it was Stefanos. Zoe turned and walked toward him, unable to prevent her boot heels from clamoring on the cobblestones. He didn't seem to mind her approach. Seagulls with wings outstretched floated in the wind just in front of him. Stefanos tossed crumbs at the birds, which they snatched up with their beaks in mid-air. Zoe found herself mesmerized by the whole spectacle of him, the birds, the sea. He wore white as the day before, but he didn't have his coat nor hat with him this time. The sea breeze ruffled his sparkling white shirt, but barely messed with his well-groomed hair. Now out of crumbs, he turned to face Zoe. His sea-blue eyes were hypnotizing, soothing, familiar. As if she'd bore witness to them before, perhaps her entire life.

"I understand you knew my grandmother well," she probed.

"Not as much as I thought I did," he replied in a gentle whisper.

"Why do you think she never mentioned this place?"

"I can't help you there, my child. There are no answers for you here. Finish your business and return home."

He bowed like a gentleman from another era and turned to leave.

"Who is Ekaterini?" she shot without thinking. The man was struck by lightning. He looked at her gravely.

"How do you know that name? Did she...?"

Zoe nodded, wondering if she was ready for the impending answer.

The man regained his composure and smiled, his eyes still incredibly captivating.

"Their secrets are written in stone. You cannot save them."

He turned and started walking away from her. She followed.

"*Secrets?* What does that mean? I need answers!"

He paid no attention to her and followed the road uphill. She let him go, her mind on the phone call she desperately needed to make.

"Who are you? I will get to the bottom of this!" she shouted after him.

FOUR
SURRENDER

1944

She ran up the hilltop, pausing on the shoulder of a rocky peak to catch her breath. She gazed across the narrow ledge towards the old, rickety hut. Concealed in the brush was the cabin her uncle Pandelis built during his youth. The structure was not visible from below, but it offered a breathtaking view of the northern end of Petra. Uncluttered by other islands, the vast blue of the Aegean disappeared into the distant horizon. Few people knew of the hut's existence. They were safe for now. It was their hiding nest.

She caught herself running every time she climbed up here, a pang of worry always burning her stride. She sighed, relieved at the sight of him, seeing him toiling away in the tiny garden. Her uncle Pandelis' old shirt and tired work pants hardly made the Nordic man look Greek. And with his striking features and grace in his manners, he looked uniquely different from anyone else she knew. She held onto her saddlebag and with her heartbeat diminishing its gallop, she walked the ledge toward him. He didn't see her coming until she cast her shadow on the tomato plants.

"I brought us some figs," she affirmed, pushing forward her bag.

She looked pretty in her long skirt with flower patterns. A blue scarf neatly tied around her hair accentuated her allure.

"We will need some sticks here," he responded, pointing at the budding leaves. "Once the tomatoes start to grow out, they will need support to stay upright to carry the fruit."

She walked around the vegetable patch and took a seat on a makeshift bench.

"They've stopped searching for us," she uttered. "Rita told me. They think we've left for the mainland. We're safe."

"For now."

"Yes, for now. We can sleep easier."

A month into his stay at Maria's villa, Stephan was noticed by a villager and the news spread throughout the island like wildfire. He stubbornly exercised on the veranda to regain his strength. He even chanced small outings into the garden much to her dismay. He began clearing the flowerbed of weeds, digging, softening the soil, caring for their favorite carnations. That's when he was spotted by a passerby. The two then fled up to the hills, an angry mob at their tail, led by Sophia. They had no plan as they fled for their lives until Maria remembered her small family secret; her uncle's eagle hut.

Seabirds and goats roamed the arid precipice, a rock

face that few barely climbed unless they were hunting for fowl. Even so, the hut was almost undetectable, covered by brush, moss and rock. It had been unattended for decades, the wooden walls falling apart. Considering their situation, it still managed to provide basic shelter. A tiny stove and a worm-eaten bed were the only occupants. With the help of Rita and Dimitri, they received weekly supplies, and day-by-day, they made it into a proper home.

"You don't deserve this," he reflected. There was something in his eyes that worried her. Ever since she nursed him back to life, it was as if this man was born to her. She could read him well.

"What do you mean?" she asked, expecting not to like his answer.

He shook the soil from his hands and sat on a stone opposite her.

"I will walk down to the village. I will surrender."

Her body went numb. She swallowed hard.

"You can't do that!"

"I can't keep on hiding."

"They will kill you."

"If I'm found guilty, I must face my crimes."

"It wasn't your fault!" she raised.

The Nazi Colonel had offered the Captain a choice. "Round up all the men and execute them. Otherwise, I will massacre the entire island, I will level the houses, and Petra will be wiped from memory."

He had told this story to Maria. His guilt over the choice he made was no less cushioned. And every time his wounds flared, he was ravaged by nightmares. She held him tight, whispered comforting things into his ear and in the process, losing her heart to him without even realizing it. She shot up on her feet, cheeks burning.

"I healed you. I risked my neck for you. I can't let you die like this!" she shouted.

He got up and approached her in his reserved manner.

"You are innocent, my dearest. I cannot drag you down with me. I don't want this on my conscience as well. Give me this choice, I beg of you. I want to set you free. You must live on this island. Believe me I do not wish to die. Your kindness was more than I thought possible in these dark times. But as you have shown me, miracles do happen in Petra. I must have faith and answer to its people."

He never saw the fig coming. It was big and juicy, and it burst right on his left cheekbone. He dodged the incoming ones, too. Exasperated, she flung her saddlebag on his plants and stormed into the cabin. It was not the first time she pelted him with fruit.

She was a woman he could not understand, a woman who fascinated him like no other. In this hideout, they slept together side by side, and yet they were not lovers. She had touched him plenty, tending to his endless wounds, yet he had barely witnessed a bare shoulder or naked ankle of hers. He was in awe of this fiery and unusual Fräulein, this angel that he would not dare lay a hand on. He felt guilty, burnt to his soul by the uniform that he had previously worn just months ago. He sat on the ledge overlooking the Aegean, feeling the sea breeze blowing on his face. He gnawed on some figs. It would be a while until she called him in for a supper.

Black clouds brought on rain and an early night. They huddled on the rickety bed staring at the roof, listening to the racket on the shingles. What they were really doing was trying to find a path to each other. He spoke first. In German.

"How can I keep my soul in me, so that it doesn't touch your soul? How can I raise it high enough, past you, to other things? I

would like to shelter it, among remote, lost objects, in some dark and silent place that doesn't resonate when your depths resound. Yet every-thing that touches us, me and you, takes us together like a violin's bow, which draws one voice out of two separate strings. Upon what instru-ment are we two spanned? And what musician holds us in his hand? Oh, sweetest song."

He had remembered this old poem by Rainer Maria Rilke, verses that struck a chord in him as a young man. Verses he would wait forever to recite to a woman. It was unfortunate he had them memorized only in German.

"I will walk with you to the village," she said, as if she was talking to herself. "You want to surrender to these people? Fine. But it will be done on my terms. You will let me handle it. I am the one person Sophia is afraid of. I will play all the cards I have for you. Then you're on your own."

"Alright, my dearest. Thank you," he breathed.

Sleep eluded them till the break of dawn.

FIVE
ISLAND OF SECRETS

The old general store was a nostalgic trip into the past. Adorned in solid wood furnishings, the place was stacked with wall-to-wall shelves made up of pickled goods, crates with fresh fruit and sacks filled with lentils, pasta and rice. The wooden floorboards creaked under her boots attracting the attention of the proprietor who was standing behind the counter. The old man looked at her over his glasses, giving her a welcoming nod. In all likelihood, he was Manos as the sign outside the establishment announced. White shirt, black vest, salt and pepper hair, pipe clenched in mouth... he looked the part.

"Good afternoon, ma'am," he said jovially in his impeccable English, showing his long, bright teeth. "Come in! Come in!"

He either knew who she was or she looked very much like a tourist, she thought.

"Hello! Can I use your phone?"

"Be my guest," he replied, pointing his pipe to a vintage telephone cabin in the back of the store. There were no other customers milling about, so Zoe had the store all to herself, which made her more at ease with the call she was about to make. She walked to the archaic phone booth and picked up the receiver. To her shock, she was faced with a rotary dial. It took a moment before she could remember the international code for the US and the area code for New York, as all that information was clearly stored in her smartphone, which would not power up. And it took an extra effort with her push button fingers to operate the numbers on the rotary dial. She knew Katie was probably asleep, but there was no way around it. She had warned her assistant about calls like this. Zoe dialed and then waited for the call to push through... which took forever, so it seemed. She was about to dial again when she saw Manos waving at her.

"Patience," mouthed the old man.

Satellites don't fly over Petra, she guessed. When she finally heard a ring tone Stateside, her eyes lit up. It was her first signal to the outside world in the last three days, and she so desperately needed to hear a friendly voice right now. It took a while for Katie to pick up.

"Hellooo...?" moaned Katie, through her sleepy mumble.

"Katie! It's Zoe. Wake up, wake up!"

"Oh! Hi Zoe. How are things...?" she replied. Zoe pictured her falling asleep on the receiver.

"Katie, sit up! I need to talk to you."

She turned her back to Manos for some privacy. She needed to shout a little to be heard.

"I'm up."

"Any word from Thacker?"

"He's called a couple of times. He was upset you weren't here."

"Didn't you explain to him—oh, never mind. What did he say?"

"The bank's giving you thirty days..." Then, a long pause.

"Jeez," Zoe felt a shiver up her spine. This train wreck has been a long time coming and now the lights were shining bright in her eyes, paralyzing her with fear. "Zoe's Blue Jeans Shoppe" would not even exist if it weren't for Yiayia's initial capital. Well-married, Grandma Maria was a well-to-do widow who always supported her granddaughter's dreams no matter how trite or lofty. Just a short train ride from the city, Zoe's boutique on Ditmars Boulevard in Astoria, Queens, provided stylish fashions for well-heeled skater punks and eclectic fashionistas at reduced prices. Boasting a curated selection of branded apparel and footwear ranging from Vans, Adidas, Nike and beyond, her store amassed a cult following that had powered it for almost a decade. But it wasn't easy. There was a shit ton of hard work behind the dream. The store's eventual success drew business from the five boroughs and beyond, then the neighborhood got hot, and so did the rents. The uphill struggle would be lost, so a bank loan seemed unavoidable.

Zoe laid her palm on her forehead, like she did so many times before. It was an attribute she had picked up from her mother.

"I'm sorry, Yiayia," she mumbled.

"Say what? Zoe...?" Katie shouted from the other end.

"Katie. Look. I'm working on a plan that can possibly save our asses. But I'll have to stay a little longer…"

Zoe caught something in the corner of her eye. Sophia was in the store and she was leaning on Manos. What was she doing here? Zoe wondered. The man looked like he was on the defensive as Sophia whispered intensely in his ear. Zoe turned her attention to the phone.

"And how was business yesterday?" she asked, her mind racing.

"Slim pickings, you know. It was a Monday, so..." she apologized. "But I got a call from Jeffrey! Our new website will soon be up and running."

"Great! I'll call you back as soon as I have more news. Tell Thacker to hold on a bit longer."

By the time Zoe hung up, Manos was now standing alone behind the counter with no trace of Sophia. She approached the old man, face in her purse.

"How much?"

"It's on the house," he said matter-of-factly.

"No, please..." she retorted, completely caught off guard.

"Your money's no good here," he insisted, pushing her wallet away. "I know who you are. I cannot charge the granddaughter of the woman who saved my life."

"My grandma saved your life?!"

"During the war. I was a partisan. Maria warned me about a German ambush. She saved my life and the lives of many others. She was a saint."

This was exciting news and she listened with her mouth wide open. "Bravo Yiayia," Zoe said to herself.

"But you must join me for a drink," demanded Manos, filling two shooter glasses. "Raki. I make it myself. Old family recipe... To your health!" he declared, raising his glass.

"Ya mas!" she joined.

They downed the drinks. Zoe got unabashedly flushed.

"And I thought the local brandy was something," she coughed, tapping her chest.

"It lifts your spirits and never gives you a hangover," he stated, biting down on his pipe with the corner of his mouth.

"I'd like to ask you something..." she continued. "How do I go about selling my grandma's villa?"

"You're selling Maria's villa?" he choked, squinting his eyes and puffing his smoke. He took a beat. "It's a bit tricky in these parts," he added, scratching his chin. "Let me ask my grandfather... he knows better about these things."

She looked at him with serious eyes, suspended in disbelief, until he cracked a smile.

"It's a local joke," he chuckled.

She smiled and nodded.

"Good one."

"Find the title deed, then get the mayor to sign off," he added.

"Right. Deed first, then mayor's signature. Thank you."

Manos poured a second serving, which she obliged, this time avoiding a succession of coughs.

"But be careful what you look for. Nothing in life is free," he added, pointing his pipe's end at her.

With the raki knocking at her senses, she listened to his warning and humored him by nodding her head many times. She forced a polite smile and ambled over to the entrance only to have her way blocked by incoming customers. They were three of them; two men and a woman. *Foreigners*, she thought immediately, easily recognizable by their sun sensitive pink complexion with matching white linen shirts and pants. But they didn't *feel* like tourists. They carried empty, re-usable shopping bags. They looked at Zoe with utter surprise and a hint of discomfort.

"Welcome!" Manos invited.

They got to work, stocking up on supplies. Zoe gestured a salute and exited the store while the three strangers kept burning her a stare.

As she walked away, the encounter buzzed in her head. There was something familiar about those people, something obvious; as if she had met them before. She couldn't quite put her finger on it. "It must be the raki," she thought.

She favored the sunny side of the street until she seized a rippling shadow motion on the cobblestones, which made her stop dead in her tracks, a sizeable flowerpot exploding inches from her feet. Shards of pottery hit her as she jumped back in shock. Zoe looked up, her eyes checking the rooftops, windows and balconies. Other flowerpots filled the ledges, but she couldn't find the missing spot. She had avoided a serious head injury, or worse, by a mere step. Wouldn't that be something? she thought with a sinking feeling. What an odd end to her journey that would have been. *The granddaughter who died during her grandmother's funeral.* For sure, that would have gone viral on the Internet. The street was empty, so there were no witnesses. That was an accident, right? Why would it be *intentional?* she asked herself. With her body tingling, she started down the street again. Ten seconds later, she heard the joyous singing emanating from the town square.

As Zoe returned to the feast, Nikos stood at the center of the plaza belting out a melancholic song while a musician backed him up on a bouzouki. The rest of the mourners followed along in unison:

"What is this thing called love? What is it? That secretly drives our hearts and whoever felt it, is nostalgic. Laughter, tear, sunshine, rain, our life, our ending and our beginning…"

These were probably the only Greek words Zoe could recognize. It was a song that her mother loved. Cleopatra would seat Zoe alongside her on the couch to watch that movie, the one where Sophia Loren sings the lyrics in Greek. She would look at her mom's reactions as she listened, watching her casually wipe away a tear. Her mother's nostalgia for some Greek-ness really left an impression on Zoe.

Her eyes fell on Paris. He reciprocated and kept looking at her as they listened to Nikos.

"Never, never has a mouth ever found it and ever said it yet. In a second, it gives you wings and it is sadness together with joy. What is this thing called love? What is it? When it makes you sing the verse, I love you, I love you, I love you."

She asked herself, "How did the songwriter know?" Overwhelmed by the moment, Zoe's unfortunate mishap just minutes ago was already a fading memory. Then it hit her! Sophia was not here and nowhere to be seen. Before she could make additional assumptions about the falling flowerpot skinning her by the teeth, Zoe realized Rita was seated just a few chairs over listening to Nikos crooning away. She immediately walked over.

Zoe took Sophia's empty seat, much to Rita's joy.

"Darling! Come, let's drink," the petite woman chirped, filling two glasses from her wine decanter. After Manos' raki, Zoe wondered how she could brave a full gulp of wine. Rita emptied her glass, which obviously wasn't her first. She began talking before Zoe could utter a word.

"You look't so much like you grandma. As if I sittin' with her right now. Like ol' times. Maria and me was like sisters. I loved her very much. I want to tell you sometin'... is heavy on my chest all these years..." Rita filled and downed another glass as Zoe sat at the edge of her seat. "Maria had special *gift*... D'you know she could see the future? Yes, yes, she read coffee cups like no one. She predict Sophia marry Nikos. Sophia not believe at first—stuck-up she was—and Nikos being just a taverna owner... But there they are, see! She also predict that Dimitri was love of my life. And that was true. But someone lies to me. They tells me that Dimitri had slippt' me love potion; potion Maria had made for him. This is why I fell love with him. I was young and foolish. Full with idio't pride, I believ't the lies and I marry Joseph... Sophia's cousin, may God rest his soul. He was guut man." She dabbed away some tears and downed another gulp.

"Was it Sophia that lied to you?" asked Zoe.

Rita seized Zoe's hands and hissed her words under her breath.

"Sophia no want Maria back on island. Of course we no listen to her. She was very angry..."

"But why?"

Rita seemed to be looking through Zoe, to a distant horizon.

"Love was different back then. It had *power*. Time stood still when you met love of your life. Like you could live forever. Me, it was Dimitri. Maria knew... Oh ya, she knew..."

Zoe seized the opportunity.

"What about Stefanos? Maria and Stefanos?" she asked.

"Stefanos was love of her life."

"Why did she leave the island?"

Rita glazed over.

"Maria didn't—"

Then her mouth froze open, her eyes fixed over Zoe's shoulder. Zoe turned and realized that the hawk woman had returned to the feast. Rita turned her back to Zoe and buried her face in her wineglass. Zoe got up on Sophia's approach.

"What a day this must be for you," she disparaged, with a tinge of a snicker.

"Yes, indeed. I'm exhausted. I'll have to excuse myself

from the festivities I'm afraid," she answered as sturdily as she could. The town square began spinning around her.

"Would you like me to walk you home?" offered Sophia.

"No, thank you. I will manage. We'll talk tomorrow."

"Yes. Tomorrow we will talk business. I may have found you a buyer for the villa."

"Sure."

Zoe did a short round to explain her departure to Father Michael and others before leaving. She noticed Paris' absence, which was best, as she was feeling quite tipsy.

Zoe paused outside the villa's door, about to search her purse for the key.

"There are no locks on the islands," she muttered. She smiled as she pushed the door open.

"*Nothing to hide?*" asked no one.

"I don't know about that... haaa!" she snickered.

Zoe was drunk. She made her way straight into the kitchen and poured herself a big glass of water, guzzling it back to the last drop. She was also hungry, the counter full of figs. She was never keen on them, but she could eat anything right now. She yanked the hard stem from a fruit and bit into it, skin and all. It tasted amazing! Her mind buzzed from the discovery of nature's natural sweetness. She gobbled down figs with delight, ignoring the mess she was making. Zoe wiped herself with her hands and tried some more, this time carefully skinning them. Energized by the sugary rush, she felt like exploring the villa.

She toured the ground floor not leaving a single shelf or cabinet unexplored.

"If I was a property deed, where would I be?" she shouted to the high ceilings.

A stateroom, a kitchen, a storeroom, a powder room and a small balcony that lead to a weed-infested patio was the general layout of the ground floor. She found a stuffed owl perched on a mount inside the storeroom atop a box that contained a phonograph and a collection of vintage vinyl records. Zoe carried them out, dusted them off, and arranged them in the living room.

Two bedrooms, a bathroom and an office completed the upper floor. The small office was bedecked with a dust-covered desk and rows of empty shelves. She also discovered a metallic vintage military trunk fastened with a giant padlock. She toyed with the lock, but had no success in opening it. At that point, Zoe felt really tired.

"I'll deal with you tomorrow," she vowed, returning to her bedroom.

She needed a proper sleep. It was early in the evening, but she didn't care. She took off her boots and began unbuttoning her shirt. On the third button, she stopped. Her eyes widened, her shoulders perked up. Those three tourists in Manos' store... she now remembered who they were! Could she be wrong, though? But then she quickly calculated the odds. If she was wrong about one of them, then how could she possibly be wrong about all three? She was not very involved in international politics, but one of the three, she believed, was the spitting image of a former British Prime Minister. And one of them looked like a famous Hollywood actor whose life was cut tragically short. The third one she couldn't remember, but he was an equal to the others. So what did it all mean? Instead of an answer, Zoe produced a yawn and she let gravity pull her down onto the sheets. Somehow she knew that Petra and her secrets would just have to wait for her till morning.

SIX
BROKEN CLOCK

1944

He had never stepped inside Saint Peter's during his two-year stay on Petra. But now, Stephan was being stared down by the stern faces of Orthodox saints gilding the church's walls. His bitter guilt bubbled in his chest, strengthening his resolve to finally be judged. Maria paced around him like a caged animal, stopping every few seconds to glance outside the stained glass windows.

"They have guns," she announced.

"There's no point hiding. I shall meet them outside," he insisted.

"Be patient."

Before he could say anything, Father Cyril returned to the church. The elder priest looked exasperated. He wiped his sweat with a large handkerchief.

"I tried my best. Sophia has them by their throats. I can barely keep them from storming this place and burning it down to the ground."

"I will go out," commanded Maria. "I will deal with her."

"It's pointless for me to hide in here. This must end…" continued Stephan, but her actions halted his intentions.

"Yes, this must end *now*!" she roared, clenching her fists. "You wait here…"

She stormed out of the church. Stephan ran to the windows, getting a distorted image of the town square through the thick glass. He turned his attention to the winding staircase on the side of the inner sanctum that ascended to the bell clock tower.

Sophia had brought the entire island with her. All the surviving Greek partisans were there, rifles in hand and bullet belts crossing their chests. She stood up front, fists on her hips, sporting a venomous look. Maria and Sophia lined up like duelists on the verge of cutting each other apart.

"Get your Nazi sweetheart out here," Sophia commanded.

"He's not responsible for the killings!" thundered Maria, looking at all of them, one by one.

"I was there. We all were!" growled Sophia. "We witnessed the execution."

"Captain Mueller did not give the order."

"Tell that to my father. Tell that to my brothers George and Panos and to their families. Tell that to the dozens of others. Your Nazi picked them for the wall."

Nikos stood behind Sophia, his rifle idling down.

"You saw Colonel Krause, too," pleaded Maria. "He ordered thirty-three of our people to be killed. The Captain had to obey or all of us would have been massacred. I'm sorry for your father and brothers, Sophia. I really am. But whom would you have Stephan pick instead? Nikos? Your young nephews? I, too, had my share of losses from this war. We all did. And I also saved the lives of many of you. Shame."

"He's guilty!" Sophia spat.

Maria ignored her and scanned the expressions of the others. They were weary of it all. Being led to hatred by Sophia's wrath. They knew, Sophia knew it, too.

"The dead demand justice," insisted Sophia.

Maria looked deeply into her eyes, unafraid. She raised her hand, thumb and middle finger joined, and made a circle in mid-air. A pang of fear sunk into Sophia's face.

"You know what the dead want, do you?" mocked Maria. "The dead are here, right now, with us, and I know what they want... They want peace, but you don't let them rest. The dead do not hate. If you commit this crime in their name, you will curse yourself, and worse, you will curse the entire island."

Nikos looked to his wife, tried to reason with her. "Maybe she's right..." which was all he could muster.

"Hold your tongue!" yelled Sophia, raising her accusing finger to Maria. "Your love for that monster is a scourge to the memory of those who were murdered in cold blood. In the name of all that is pure, I curse you, Maria Artemisou and Stephan Mueller! May your days be a never ending torment, and may the people of Petra live forever!"

This proclamation sent shivers up the spines of all those present. Even Maria fell silent.

Suddenly, one of the men pointed to the bell tower and shouted.

"Up there! I see him!"

They all looked up. Stephan was on the gallery leaning onto the church's bell, watching. Sophia turned and snatched Nikos' rifle out of his hand and before anyone could react, she fired at the tower. Maria shrieked as the bullet hit the bell. The ricochet produced a sad toll and

Stephan collapsed holding his face. Maria ran back into the church as Nikos wrestled his rifle from Sophia.

She reached the top of the tower and found him crouched down on the gallery, bleeding by his left temple. She yelled out his name and fell to her knees, pulling him into her arms.

"I'm okay. It's just a scratch," he downplayed.

She cupped his face with her hands and looked at his wound. Her eyes then landed on his and she couldn't let go. Their lips met, their embrace tightened. They had no words for each other. They did not need words. The affection was there; it had been for a long while. And it defied explanation. She had seen this moment in her coffee cup. So, who was she to refuse the gods? In their kiss, they abandoned the rest of the world. They even missed the growling of the earth's thunder.

The ground shook hard. Petra had not experienced this magnitude of earthquake since Ancient Times. The people in the town square squealed and rolled to the ground, swallowed by shooting dirt. The clock tower shook and the bell tolled chillingly. Its walls started to crack, splitting the mortar and showering the villagers with clouds of dust. The inner workings of the clock moaned as they twisted and popped. Rooftop tiles smashed onto the cobblestones, fracturing into thousands of bits. People scurried away, fearful for their lives. Only Sophia remained in place, standing tall and fearless. Nikos cowered behind her.

When it was all over, Maria and Stephan opened their eyes and unlocked their lips. They beamed with lust and lament, bearing the weight of infinite defeated loves that never saw the light of day.

They awakened to a different Petra.

SEVEN
SUDDEN DEPARTURE

The full moon glowed majestically over a slumbering Petra. Stefanos stepped out of his tiny house in the dead of night all gussied up. After all, he was the star attraction for what would transpire next.

He closed the door behind him and started his descent to the bottom of the village following the oft-trotted path of donkeys and mules. He had mastered his footing on this ridge after so many years that he could descend it with his eyes closed. This particular walk was long overdue, and the night seemed to agree with him. He whistled an old tune, to which a sleepy owl chortled back.

When the stumped grass changed to paved road he paused and turned his attention to Maria's villa. *Finally*, he thought. The house was breathing life again. He had dreamt about this day for so long, at one point he even stopped believing that it would ever happen. He smiled, removed his hat and pressed it to his chest. He felt the breath of the night brushing his hair behind his ear, like a gentle kiss from an angel. The village was dark but the cobblestones shone blue, leading him all the way to the harbor. He was in no hurry, though. He strolled down with a luxury he never had before. He had cared for two people in all his life, their memory now a thorn in his heart. But tonight, it was a celebration. A long missed reunion.

Stefanos stood on the pier and listened to the sea licking the breakwall under his feet. Without thinking, he chose to get into Elias' boat. Of all the islanders, Elias was the one person that would show him some understanding, he thought. He and the fisherman had shared more than a carafe of ouzo together throughout the years. Stefanos was just borrowing his vessel temporarily, long enough to get to the other side. He carefully climbed down the iron ladder, hopped onto the vessel and untied the rope that held the boat, pushing away the pier. He sat down and took hold of the oars with his back turned to the stern. Stefanos began to row away from the island. He would soon have the whole of Petra in his sights, a dark mass under a glorious moon. He pulled the oars out of the water, laid down at the bottom of the boat, and rested his hat on his chest. The canopy above him was full of sparkling stars. He smiled. He was in high spirits. Gentle waves rocked the keel, as he eventually closed his eyes and slipped soothingly into the cosmos.

~

Zoe had no alarm clock, but the dawn's early light was strong enough to push her out of bed. This incredible Greek light, once it touched the sky, would not let her sleep another wink.

She paced all over the villa, downing a bitter cup of Greek coffee. She decided she had to buy some sugar and additional supplies from Manos. Zoe took herself for a lazy morning riser, an illusion quickly shattered the moment she dragged herself out of the villa and onto the veranda. The power of the glorious Greek sun instantaneously warmed her bones, burst open her appetite and set her sniffer on fire. She smelled juniper and chamomile, oregano and mint. She then got a whiff of oven-baked bread and freshly squeezed orange juice seeping from homes down below in the village. The fragrances from the flowerbed on the left corner of her magnificent garden—which oddly enough, she hadn't spotted before—were next on her tasting menu. It was overflowing with tall, blossoming red carnations and she wondered aloud to herself, "Nice job! Who's the green thumb around here?" Her senses were erupting. Then it dawned on her. Two days into her visit and Zoe still hadn't been properly introduced to the island of Petra. And like a typical New Yorker whose biggest fear is "missing out", she didn't skip a beat. She popped inside, donned on her multi-colored yoga wear, laced up her Nikes and ran out the door.

She jogged down the road, coming across the everyday hustle and bustle of the village. She also realized she had neglected her exercises for a long while. On a good day, she could cover about sixteen miles from the top of Central Park over the Triborough Bridge to Randall's Island to Queens and back. She figured she could probably run around Petra more than once, doing some exploring in the process. There were locals on the streets—not many children or young people—mostly elders in their daily toils. None used a cane, nor a walker, nor dragged their feet. They all looked deceivably cheerful and perky. Most smiled and waved at her. She waved back as she kept running, feeling a bit self-conscious about her buoyant appearance. Zoe was still the protagonist of this Greek movie, the villagers fixating their attention on her. She noticed the horse-drawn carriage that had picked up

Maria's coffin from the pier days earlier. Today it was delivering blocks of ice door-to-door, and *how odd was that?* She was frustrated that her smartphone was malfunctioning, which meant she was missing tons of photo opps. Social media would just have to wait a few days, she humored. Who needs "Likes" when she's actually liking what she's seeing!

Unlike the previous two days, shutters and windows were now open, bed sheets and other linens hung out to dry. And she could hear music, laughter, rowdy conversations, and spats vibrating from inside the homes. She arrived at the farmer's market at the town square. Dozens of counters with fresh goods were plunked in a grid with a true menagerie of appetizing colors made up of local eggplants, cucumbers, tomatoes, peppers and exotic fruits. Even Aaron was there with a shopping bag still wearing the same get-up, sniffing peaches and haggling with fervor. Zoe observed that very little coin exchanged hands. It was mostly a barter system—like three eggs for three tomatoes—kind of trading. Rita sat behind her own counter, displaying bunches of zucchinis. She spotted Zoe and waved her over.

"Good mornin', darling!" hooted the cheery woman in her broken, by lovable English. "How you this morning?"

"Okay, I guess. I'm having trouble finding the deed to the villa," Zoe answered.

"No worry, you will find," added Rita, smiling reassuringly.

"You know where I can find a notary?"

Rita frowned, perplexed.

"No notary in Petra. The notary in Andoriani."

"But Sophia said…" It was now Zoe's turn to frown. She stopped her urge to use inappropriate language.

"Never believe anytin' Sophia say," remarked Rita,

shaking her head. Then, as if a new thought burst inside her head, she looked at Zoe, smiling.

"You cook, my sweetie?" she asked.

Startled by the change of subject, Zoe found herself in a difficult place.

"No. I'm afraid not..."

"Oh dear," giggled Rita, covering her cheeks. "No good to findin' husband. Look what I have here... You know these?"

She lifted a plastic bag from the back of her chair and held it for Zoe to look inside. She could not recognize the contents.

"Zucchini flowers!" explained Rita. "You deep fry or stuff with rice in oven... sooo delicious! I'll make't for you, you lick your fingers, yes?"

Zoe smiled and nodded. Suddenly, a distant shout pierced the market, which soon escalated to jibber-jabber, reaching each resident, mouth-to-ear. Now everyone was repeating the news and all Zoe could understand were the shocked expressions on the villagers' faces. Without warning, the church bell rang a listless and morose toll, instantly silencing the crowd. Zoe's eyes shot up to the bell clock tower and noticed Paris chiming the bell. He looked quite distraught. He swallowed hard, holding back tears. She turned to Rita, whose lips trembled uncontrollably.

"What's wrong?"

"Stefanos is dead!"

Stefanos' house was a ten-minute walk from Maria's villa. Following Rita's instructions, Zoe made it there in a flash with her jogger's stride. It was a typical Dodecanesian stone dwelling, facing the backside of the island. It stood alone with no neighbors, on top of a cliff that tumbled all the way down to the northern shore. A strong sea wind whipped Zoe and it wasn't hard for her to imagine what it must be like in wintertime. The house was whitewashed with lilac shutters and doors, very picturesque but "sad" as she thought to herself. Why did Yiayia's lover live up here alone, but yet so close to her villa? Zoe stepped in closer, carrying an offering of figs. The front door was open and on the porch was an old gentleman in a wheelchair. As she approached, his eyes and friendly smile greeted her. He was one more striking example of Petra, a strapping elderly lad. *Levendis*, being the proper Greek word.

"Welcome," he said in old English.

"Am I early?" she asked, pausing in front of him.

"Time has no meaning here. You can never be too early or too late in Petra... You're Maria's granddaughter?"

"Yes. Am I the first one, then?"

"There will be no wake. Stefanos left specific instructions. He will be buried today next to his love."

She felt awkward in front of this stranger.

"What happened? How did he?—"

The man raised his shoulders.

"He waited long enough. It was his time for my good friend to go. That is all."

She turned away, her mind racing on what to do next. So many questions unanswered.

"Would you like to come in?" he asked.

She looked at him, startled.

"You have every right. Go inside and look around. You'll discover nice mementos. Although I'm sorry to say, I didn't get here soon enough. I saw Sophia leaving with bags of loot, that witch."

A touch of anger flared in her cheeks.

"Sophia was here??"

"Yes. I cursed her, but she ran away. What could I do?" he sighed, pointing to his wheelchair.

She moved toward the open door, paused and extended her hand to him.

"I'm Zoe," she revealed.

"I know," he replied, taking her hand and kissing it. "You are as beautiful as Maria was. I am Dimitri."

"You're Rita's Dimitri?" she blurted out, surprised.

He laughed.

"I wish I was. Rita… she's my little dove. She's under the claws of that hawk these days," he ached. Right then, Zoe knew she would like this man.

The house was clean and tidy, sparse in its décor with only the absolute essential furnishings. Zoe left her offering of figs on the bare kitchen table. There were a few dishes and cups in the cupboard of the kitchen, its sink spotless. The kitchen door led to a tiny garden outside that was well protected by the winds. Zoe noticed a significant bed of blooming carnations. The rest of the home featured a single bed in a modest living room with sheets and covers tightly wrapped around its mattress. The most striking feature of the place, the one that took Zoe's breath away, were the photographs. On desktops and on the walls, the photos displayed a long chapter of Yiayia's life that her granddaughter was completely unaware of. There was Maria on frames; young, beautiful, happy, next to the love of her life, a younger Stefanos.

They were both smiling and posing in front of the Coliseum in Rome, Big Ben in London, and Notre-Dame in Paris. A bitter memory stung Zoe as she remembered her mother, Patra. Zoe's mom never forgave Maria for not truly loving her dad. This subject would come up every time her mother and grandmother had one of their fiery arguments, which happened a lot. And there were those times when Zoe sat with her mom in the kitchen, Patra drinking and chain-smoking, blurting out accusations into thin air. Patra would say that her dad took that bitter pill with him to his grave. Looking at the picture frames, Zoe could now make sense of it all. If Yiayia loved a man like Stefanos, how much of herself would she have left to give to someone else?

She looked at the edges of the photographs, trying to locate dates, but there were none. Maybe they had stamps in the back, but she would have to ask Dimitri's permission to open up the frames. In the tidiness of the small living room, one jarring glitch was a cabinet drawer that was left open. She approached to have a look-see without touching anything. The drawer was neatly stacked with stationery, pens and pencils, a box of paperclips, a passport, plus other legal documents. In one corner, among other knickknacks, stood an empty spot, which meant something had just gone missing from there. Something hastily removed, Zoe pondered.

"Sophia..." she thought.

She returned to the porch to find Dimitri waiting for her.

"When did my Yiayia and Stefanos leave the island?"

"You are in a hurry to find answers."

"I'm running out of time."

"Oh," he reacted in a mock dramatic gesture. "Out of time on Petra?"

"Look..." she tried to collect her thoughts. "I have a business back home—"

"This is your home—"

"My business in New York is in trouble, and I need to get back soon. I must settle all that's left here and quick."

She wondered if she was making any sense at all to this man.

"You want to sell the villa... Does Sophia approve?" he asked, with a mocking expression.

"Really. Who's this Sophia? What's the deal with her?"

The distant, sad toll of the church bell reached their ears.

"It's time to put our friend to rest," sniffled Dimitri.

Zoe hung her shoulders and sighed. Dimitri took her hands in his, looked her in the eyes.

"I know you think you have this *trouble*... But be patient. Do not hurry. Stay a while. Let Petra talk to you. You'll find all the answers, and then you'll know what is truly important."

Even if it was difficult to agree with him, she smiled gently.

"Let us go now," he said.

The plot next to Yiayia Maria's grave was untouched just yesterday. It was now dug six feet deep, and it welcomed Stefanos' casket. Kostas, the gravedigger and local carpenter, had already taken care of business. He looked exhausted, stood solemnly over the hole, leaning white-knuckled against his shovel. Zoe was surprised by the lack of attendance at the funeral service, evidenced by only a handful of islanders scattered about the grave plot. She had Dimitri and Rita on opposite sides of her, the two of them amusingly exchanging glances.

Across from Father Michael stood a new person; a woman in her mid-thirties that Zoe was seeing for the very first time. She wore khaki overalls and hard terrain shoes. She was pretty, with a long blonde mane and striking facial features. Zoe assumed she was one of the foreigners living on the island enjoying its Blue Zone benefits. She looked genuinely distraught and Zoe wondered what the connection was between this woman and Stefanos. It was probably best to ask questions after the funeral, to get straight answers, Zoe surmised. But her curiosity just couldn't wait!

And of course, the entire party of mourners also served as pallbearers. Paris was at his father's side, assisting with the service. Zoe couldn't help but notice how mournful he too looked. But her gaze was short-lived, as the unknown blonde woman gave Zoe the hairy eyeball, immediately making her turn away. Zoe dared not shoot her back a dirty look. After all, she was a fish out of water and she was mindful enough not to cause any unnecessary waves. Certainly not today. Not at a funeral.

When the last dusting of earth was tossed into the grave, Zoe walked toward the priest-in-training. To her surprise, Paris saw her coming and he took a quick step back before turning to march hurriedly away. Zoe remained in mid-step, dumbfounded by his behavior.

"No mind him, darling," Rita gossiped by her side. "Sophia make't him crazy all morning."

"What she say to him?" asked Zoe.

"She just terrible. Good with lies," divulged Rita, dismissing any further commentary with a wave of her hand. She smiled and blushed as Dimitri approached.

"Hello beautiful!" he swooned at Rita. "Do we need funerals to meet?"

"You no visit this side of island," she retorted, still speaking English for Zoe's sake.

"Well, here I am," he answered, winking at her. "My

buddy left me and now I'm all alone up there on the northern side. You might get used to seeing more of me…"

"I only wish."

"In fact, I've decided to take over Stefanos' house—"

"Finally some guut news!"

"Up for a stroll, my beauty?"

She curtsied and moved behind his wheelchair, grabbing hold of the handles.

"We must talk soon," Dimitri revealed to Zoe, as Rita whisked him out of the cemetery.

The unknown woman strode to the gate as if being chased. Before Zoe could reach her, Father Michael cut in.

"Is Paris okay?" she asked him, watching the woman disappear down the path.

"He understands that Stefanos is with God now, but he is… sensitive with losing friends. He and Stefanos go way back."

"Well, it was a beautiful service, Father. But I feel as though I brought death to the island."

"Nonsense, my child," he insisted, resting his hand on her shoulder. "That is Sophia talking…" Father Michael fell silent, embarrassed, feeling as though he said something unfitting.

"Oh?" reacted Zoe. "What else does Sophia talk about?"

"Ignore and forgive our peasant folk, my daughter. They have unconventional ways of seeing things. Let us make peace between us. You are invited for dinner at my home tonight. I will cook in your honor."

"Thank you. That will be lovely, Father. What time?"

He smiled.

"When the sun is almost set and the sky gets dark pink... That will be appropriate."

"I see," she nodded, her eyes falling on her stopped wristwatch. She shook it to no avail.

She didn't expect to still be on the island. One piece of luggage was all she had brought. She had only one remaining folded outfit left, which she intended to use for her return trip; a pair of cream pants, a green shirt and a colorful neck handkerchief. She took a shower and then wandered the rooms in her underwear, drinking some left-over brandy. Out of curiosity, she yanked some of the remaining drop sheets from covered furniture, revealing wooden antique tables and big sofas. On her way to dinner, she would stop at Manos' for a bottle of wine. She didn't want to show up empty-handed. She would also call Katie and let her know about the new delay.

EIGHT
ESCAPE

1947

She ran uphill as always, was out of breath and anxious until she reached their old shack. They had no use for it now, but Stephan would escape here every so often, finding solace in its nature. He would fiddle with his tools, fix broken boards and loose hinges—anything to take his mind away from the toxicity of the village. She knew he endured all of it for her and she loved him even more for it. Maria had many islanders on her side, but they were few compared to those who still carried grudges from the occupation. They kept mostly to themselves inside her villa, chancing long walks on remote parts of the island in the off-hours.

Stephan had his back to her and she treaded softly toward him as he removed rusty nails from the door. He felt her presence and turned to face her.

"How was it?" he asked, leaving his hammer down.

"Not as many candles as you predicted on the cake!" she replied, smiling and winking. "He didn't look a day past one hundred. Hard to imagine he was at death's door just two years ago."

"Well, was he happy...?"

"Yes, he was! 102 and you should have seen him dance."

He backed off, went to lift a shingle from the stack by the door. He didn't want her to see his disappointment, she guessed. Kostas was a good friend, but the rest of his guests at his birthday party would have seen red if Stephan had shown up.

"I have news," she added. "We got ourselves a boat. Kostas' nephew, Argyris, will cross us to the mainland. It's time," she continued, waiting for his reaction.

There were clouds in his eyes.

"Are you sure you want to leave Petra?" he asked.

"I don't want to stay here. Not anymore. I see death wherever I look," she affirmed. The war in Europe had ended. But the young men of Petra that had survived were now being conscripted into the Royal Army to fight a civil war in the mountains of Greece—a war that was tearing the country apart. "I see dreams, I see signs... We'll become like them if we stay any longer. I'm not happy here," she almost shouted.

He stopped working and inched closer to her.

"Love lives... but so does hate. They won't let go. Let us leave this place," she begged.

"Where shall we go?"

"Anywhere. We will make a life elsewhere. I do not want to start a family here."

He nodded.

"All right, mein Liebling. All right," he exhaled.

They embraced, and the rest of the world just disappeared.

NINE

THE CLOCK TINKERER AND THE MAIDEN

As Zoe walked to Manos' store, the slow setting sun touched the sea and a golden hue brushed over Petra, enhancing the evening colors into an unimaginable dream-like canvas. And for that fleeting moment, it looked more real than her life in New York. Even her daily phone calls with Katie echoed so distantly, like she was conversing with her past and irrelevant life. Zoe convinced herself that her stay on the island would be extended until she resolved the sale of her grandmother's villa. At times, she even heard panic in her assistant's voice who suddenly had to manage the store on her own. She gave Katie soothing assurances, uttering words that surprised even Zoe. Where was her usual New Yorker anxiety? Did she really become that hopeful all of a sudden? Could this place hold that much power over her? She was on Petra just a mere moment, she reflected.

Manos sat behind his counter, downing shots of raki and clutching a letter to his chest when she approached. And this time she was determined to make him accept payments for her calls when she noticed tears on his cheek.

"Are you all right?" she asked.

He smiled and self-consciously wiped his cheek clean.

"Just being sentimental, is all," he said. "I received a letter from my grandson. He just completed his military service. He and his fiancée are planning to get married and they've decided to host the ceremony here on the island."

"That's wonderful!"

"Yes, it is. I am very proud of him and I have missed him, of course. He does not visit much. His job is in Athens… with his father."

"Your son?"

Manos nodded.

"You'd like to see them more often, huh?" Zoe queried, worried she may have stepped on sensitive ground.

"Petra's not a place for young people." He shrugged.

"What about you? You could visit them?"

He downed one more shot and looked at her with dopey eyes.

"Yes, I could. What could stop me, right...?"

They found a bottle of red wine on a back shelf coated with thick dust, explaining that she was invited over to Father Michael's. Manos assured her this wine was the best he had, that it came from a reputable winery on Andoriani. And of course he gave it to her at no cost. Zoe declined to accept the bottle at first without swapping it for money. But as the story repeated itself, Manos' charm and charisma were no match for hers.

She witnessed the vibrant life of the village on her way to Father Michael's. Completely undeterred by the sinking daylight, Zoe spotted house doors open, tables and chairs propped at the steps, locals lounging and chatting with their neighbors. Mr. Fanouris was chain-smoking and twirling his amber-beaded komboloi (Greek rosary), his gaze lost in the sky. He was listening attentively to a gathering of old ladies in the adjoining garden who were singing some traditional folk songs. One house over, Chrysoula sat on her steps, knife in hand and a bowl of okra on her knees. She started cutting the hard stems off. "Grandparents without grandchildren," Zoe mused. With all its picturesque beauty, the one thing that was missing on Petra was the noisy presence of children, she thought.

"They play in the streets and alleyways, free of concern, raising a racket, ignoring the calls of their mothers until late into the evening, they return to their homes with torn clothes and bloody knees... And they are happy." Stories Zoe's mom would tell her about Greece while explaining the reasoning behind why she was being raised away from the grayness of the city. Saratoga Springs had its country charms but in no way touched the magic of the Greek countryside. Zoe's mom, Patra, had never traveled to Greece. She was speaking from hearsay, her whole life trying to get in touch with her heritage much more so than Zoe's dad ever did. On their rare family outings to Astoria, Queens to pick up Greek food supplies, her father would always remark how ghetto the neighborhood was when seeing immigrant kids playing around opened fire hydrants in the streets. "America has let in the worst of the worst. Before we know it, we'll be overrun by peasants," he would say. Zoe always thought that strange. Especially considering her dad was an educated man, and a good man, to boot.

~

Father Michael's house was located behind the church, a simple whitewashed home enclosed in a box-like garden filled with fruit trees. On her approach, Zoe noticed lights on in the bell clock tower. From below, she could see a shadow moving inside. The door to the church was closed, but the scaffolding had its own separate and open entrance. She paused, dithered, and after some hesitation, she stepped in. She climbed the wooden stairs to the workshop area surrounding the big clock carefully clasping the bottle of red wine. Last thing she wanted to do was drop it and look like an idiot. Zoe saw Paris perched on a wooden gantry vigorously filing a pair of gears. He did all that while keeping his balance, yet still garbed in his priesthood gray clothes. The steps creaked under her weight, but he didn't notice her presence.

"Hi!" she shouted.

He heard her and looked down. He didn't act surprised.

"Hello," he responded, hopping off the gantry. He grabbed a rag from his tool kit and wiped grease off his hands.

As she waited for him, she spotted a big crack on the wall to her left side. She ran her fingers over it, mumbling to herself what could have caused it.

"That's from the big earthquake of 1944," he noted, now standing next to her. "Most homes on the island have scars like this."

He smiled. Zoe reacted like a smitten schoolgirl.

"I was on my way to your father's and saw you up here," she said, wondering if she had stuttered a little. She couldn't tell.

"I'm sorry for my behavior this morning," he interjected. "I was... upset."

"That's okay. I understand."

"My dad's been in the kitchen all day," he added, willfully changing his tone. "He really wants to impress you."

"If his custard pie was the preview of things to come, I'm already sold!"

She wasn't sure he understood the reference, but it didn't matter. His blue eyes shined on her, so welcoming, they both lost their train of thought. They silly smiled at each other.

"It's not very safe up here," he said. "Let's go to the tool shed below."

The tool shack was bigger inside than it looked from the village square. Filled with crates and shelves and a workbench, it bore a history of structural additions and endless slogging. In one corner, there was an open crate with piles of broken clocks. She fixed the bottle of wine on a clean, safe spot and picked up a few clocks to examine. Some were ordinary, others odd, but most looked like genuine antiques. Though none of them worked.

"What's all this?"

He leaned over a small aluminum basin where he poured water out of a pitcher, and with a bar of soap, he washed his oily hands.

"Watchmaking is a hobby," he drifted, pausing, his fixed eyes on his hands. "But also a curse."

"What do you mean?"

"Legend has it, the island's made up of a highly-charged magnetic field."

"Oh. Is this why nothing works on this island? Clocks and smartphones?"

"Do you have time for a brief history lesson?" he asked, smiling.

"Time? Nothing but... This is Petra, after all," she shot back.

"Ha. Quick learner," he grinned as he nodded. "You

see, the tectonic plates shifted Petra's magnetic field so much during the earthquake, everything just went *haywire*. After that, the government hardwired the entire island with electricity by underwater cables directly from Andoriani. That's why light bulbs, ovens, iceboxes, all work because they are simple electric circuits. Let me show you what I mean..."

He rummaged through a few boxes on the bench and produced a light bulb. He lifted a dusty lamp from a corner and plugged it into a circuit box. He then screwed the bulb on the lamp. It lit up.

"A simple light bulb on a lamp hardwired to my workshop, correct?"

She nodded, fascinated by his every move.

He then took a large magnet out of the bench drawer and held it next to the glowing bulb.

"And when I introduce a heavy magnet, it still stays lit."

Paris then removed the lamp from the power outlet and drew a large battery from under a drop cloth. He plugged the lamp into it and the bulb instantly radiated.

"But when I place the same lamp onto a direct energy source and run the same magnet near it..."

She inched closer, entranced by his delivery. Before he could bring the magnet to the bulb, it flickered and turned off. Paris smiled.

"What happened?" she asked.

"Well, the island's magnetic force is the *trick*. The battery had no chance."

"Fascinating... but I don't follow," she admitted.

"The bell clock was and is hardwired, too. Which means technically it should work, but it doesn't—"

"The clock is not a simple electric circuit," she computed.

"Something like that. It's not *that* simple... But my goal is to get it working again."

She made a devilish grin and took in a hiccup-y breath. She couldn't help but to burst out laughing.

"That's why you're tinkering with your clock all the time, huh?"

He finally got her joke, and to her delight he started laughing, too. She bit her lower lip, enamored by his wondrous laugh. She pointed to the pile of clocks.

"But most of these are wind up clocks, like my wristwatch. They tick from a compressed spring, or something. At least the expensive watches do... No battery, right?"

"It's all a mystery. All I can say is that people from all over the world send me their broken clocks. Word has gone around that Petra holds some magical, mystical power where time stands still. These poor folk think the island will bless them in some ludicrous way, hoping time will have mercy on them... I sometimes wonder who the real cuckoo is? Them? Or me, for accepting their broken hopes and dreams, none of which I can fix."

She felt a great deal of sadness oozing from his now-piercing blue eyes, which reminded her so much of Stefanos' on the last day of his life, when she spoke to him by the cliff overlooking the sea.

"I am a watchmaker with lots of time on my hands," he added, gazing at her.

She instinctively looked at her own watch.

"Here I am, another desperate case on your front step," she grinned. "It stopped working. And I insist on wearing it for sentimental reasons, of course."

"Let me have a look..."

He took her wrist in his big hands and delicately removed her watch. They looked deeply into each other's eyes and she turned beet red. She gulped, her knees almost giving out. Zoe was practically swooning, and he knew it. Right then, Paris knew he could play this to his full advantage. He seized control of the moment by looking away from her, playing hard to get, his motions deliberately smooth as silk.

"Be gentle with it. It belonged to my grandmother..."

He took a chair at his workbench and produced a magnifying glass from his shirt pocket. He examined her watch with the professionalism of a physician. He wiped the glass clean with his thumb. He looked very serious, which made Zoe smile.

"Beautiful piece. Rare, mid-century Cartier. Nice workmanship." He turned it around and examined the backside. Paris edged the watch even closer to his face.

"There's a tiny inscription that's barely visible..."

She had the watch since she was sixteen and this was news to her. She leaned in closer, awestruck by this revelation.

"I thought it was just the factory specs. Could never make out the words... What's it say?"

Decades of rub and sweat had made the writing almost unintelligible. A reflection from its silvery surface revealed a slight trace of lettering. Paris let his hand do the walking through his toolbox as he kept his eyes directed on the watch. He squirted nail polish remover on a pinch of cotton swab and wiped the grime of time off the writing, slanting the watch to the light to make out the words. He frowned. Zoe fretted.

"Pethi Mou," he read.

"Which means?"

"Well, it has two meanings. It could either mean *My Child*, or, *My Darling*..."

Yiayia Maria had given the watch to Zoe for her sweet sixteen. And it wasn't handed to her in a box, wrapped in fancy gift tissue and gilded bow. As memory served her correctly, Grandma Maria and her mother Patra had a row that evening over the girl's future while they were cutting Zoe's birthday cake. And as usual, Maria concluded her side of the issue with a grand, dramatic gesture, sliding the watch off her own wrist and clasping it onto her granddaughter's. That memory now made Zoe feel as though she were receiving this gift again for a second time. She looked sentimental, misty, ready to tear up.

Zoe noticed Paris was still scrutinizing the inscription. He lowered the watch, looking a bit perplexed.

"What is it now?" she asked.

"Nothing," he muttered, and with a shake of his shoulders he reset his face to its normal disposition.

"Give it back then," she demanded, extending her naked wrist. He tenderly approached her, and with tact, wrapped the watch around her wrist much to her hidden delight.

"Now, can I tell you a secret?" she whispered over his shoulder. His face went blank. "I don't see you as a priest..."

His lips fluttered. He cleared his throat.

"Well, the elders see it differently. They've been busy setting up my official ordination ceremony for the Big Feast, which is coming up soon. Don't want to disappoint them," he smirked.

"Not exactly what I meant," she quipped. "I think you have more choices than you think. I just don't see you living on this island forever."

"Forever is a long time on Petra," he gurgled.

Out of nowhere, an awkward pause befell them. Zoe screamed in her mind to think of something new to say.

"I think you should deck out the church walls with all

these broken clocks. The sight of them all piled up together would be… stunning."

"Stunning… You think so?"

"Yes. You should put the smaller clocks on the bottom and the bigger ones up top. Make it top-heavy. It'll make for a more striking perspective."

~

He turned off the lights in the shed before they walked out, Zoe still holding onto the bottle of red wine. The sky was dark blue with the first glimmer of stars spotting the heavenly canopy. The lights were on in Father Michael's home and an open door awaited them. Paris paused, delaying their entry into the house.

"You know what I miss the most about the mainland…?"

"What's that?" she asked without missing a beat.

"Blue jeans."

"Oh really?" she inquired, totally dumbfounded. She definitely wanted to hear some more, so she shook her head just a touch, giving him the green light he was waiting for. He looked a little naughty, like a guilty adolescent.

"I remember when I was studying at the Seminary in Athens, I would sneak out at night and wear jeans under my long black robes. I'd walk around the city for hours on end. I loved how they felt on me, how they hugged *my*…" Self-conscious, he looked at Zoe as if he wasn't expecting to go this far in his confession. "You know, my *bottom*… my behind."

She chuckled.

"They used to sell these cool jeans with white streaks in them. They were called—"

"Stone-washed," she helped.

"Yes! I loved them! They were... *amazing*," he announced, again trying his best at American speak.

"Haaa!" Zoe laughed hard, startling him.

"What? What did I say?"

She shook her head.

"Nothing. Go ahead."

"For me, they represented freedom. No one knew me in the city. I could come and go as I pleased. Here, I have to look a certain way, behave as I am told. You city people work your asses off to save enough money just to come out here to lose yourselves. I would give anything to be anonymous again, just for one day..."

She nodded and stepped close enough to rub elbows with him.

"Freedom, check. Jeans, check. I know enough on both subjects."

She locked her eyes on his, expecting him to make the first move. Just then, she was startled by a loud clang. She jumped and grabbed his arm, trying desperately not to drop the wine. Father Michael stood at the door waving a dinner bell. But he couldn't see them against the dark structure of the church. He turned around and walked back inside.

"Dinner's ready," declared Paris. They both fought hard to drown out their laughter. They cackled and gaggled, their tummies bursting with hoots and hollers. They were both hunched over now, and they couldn't stop laughing. After about half a minute, they caught their breaths. They helped each other up and resumed their walk through the front door.

"Does this happen often? Very fancy, that dinner bell..."

"Well, that was the original school bell. Back in the day when Petra still had children, my father doubled as the truant officer for the school."

"That's sad to think. That all the children are gone," she argued, now more serious.

"The children are gone because they had to follow their parents. This abandonment isn't unusual in Greece. It's more striking in Petra because it's a small island. The story repeats itself in countless remote villages on the mainland."

"Pity. This is a great place to raise children. I love the city, but I grew up in the country."

"One day the children will come back. When I fix that clock."

She looked at him puzzled.

"Let's not keep my dad waiting. I'm sure the dishes are being served as we speak," he stated, taking Zoe softly by the wrist and leading her into the house. She marvelled at his assertiveness, her eyes widening with delight.

She described the dinner spread as "divine" and even though she was tipsy from the accompanying raki, she wasn't far from the truth. She had tasted similar food as a child when her mother would occasionally cook some of Grandma's secret family recipes. Rice stuffed tomatoes and peppers, an eggplant casserole and a peppery spinach salad more than confirmed Father Michael's reputation. With their bellies now full, they sat back to enjoy their second bottle of raki, the bottle of red wine already polished off hours ago. The low-ceilinged dining room generated a warm sense of intimacy.

"You are an incredible cook, Father. Tell me again how this island's open-door policy works?" she inquired playfully.

"You have a standing reservation at this table," answered the priest, bowing his head.

"Don't tempt me. I'll have to run marathons to shed the calories."

Father Michael poured raki in their glasses.

"One more shot before I make coffee. Tell us, dear Zoe... about life in America. Tell us about Maria."

She sipped her raki, thinking about what to say. Father Michael and Paris glued their eyes on her.

"Well..." she said, wiping her lips with her thumb and collecting her thoughts. "From what I remember, Grandma never really spoke much about Petra even though she baptized my mom with the island's name. My mother wanted so badly to get in touch with her own culture, that's why she married a Greek. My father, Leonidas, was a third generation Greek American, a veterinarian, who didn't speak a word of Greek and was even more out of touch with his Greek-ness. But they fell in love much to my grandma's ire, and that was that. To add insult to injury, my father moved his practice to a small town—Saratoga Springs, New York—widening the rift between Maria and Patra. And there, I was born. Until I was six, I didn't even know I had a *yiayia*. I remember one day she appeared out of nowhere on an Easter Sunday and I was just mesmerized by this incredible woman! She was a tour de force... Sparkling and elegant. And loud! So loud... my god. She spoke her mind. I'd never seen such behavior before and I ate it all up. My father was anti-social, and my mother was reserved about everything except when it came to Grandma Maria. When those two women would meet... POW! Greekness exploded."

Zoe laughed and the men joined in.

"Loud... that we are," Father Michael commented as he got up. He made his way to the stove at the end of the room and got busy with the coffeepot.

"When did you move to New York City?" asked Paris.

"I decided immediately after my mom died, as I was graduating from high school—"

"Oh. God bless her soul. I am sorry—"

"That's all right. It's been thirteen years now... I'm over it," she said with a fake-smile. "Where was I...?"

"You were telling us about your move to the city—" Paris looking concerned for her.

"Yes!" Zoe tried to save face, gathering her thoughts. "Of course, my decision saddened my father, but with Maria's support I found the courage. I would eventually drop out of NYU and open up my very own clothing shop... and it's been a fight for survival ever since. I keep my head above water on my best days, but I have no regrets. We're launching an online market in the coming weeks, which is exciting!"

Paris sat there, clueless.

"What I meant to say was, we're creating a website to drive more clients directly to our *merch* rather than to our physical shop. Because we all know brick and mortar is just plain suicide these days, right...?"

Her references missed the mark once more. Father Michael returned to the table with a tray of steaming coffee cups.

"Truthfully. I just fool people into buying clothes they don't really need at inflated prices," she continued, Paris making a weird face at her. "Even blue jeans on occasion," she joked, which didn't really ease his mood. Zoe rubbed her palm on her nose. "Don't pay attention to me. I think I'm drunk."

She took a sip of Greek coffee as a distraction and kept the cup in her hands.

"Well, it's nice to keep busy with something you are passionate about," Father Michael said, trying to sound sympathetic. She smiled gratefully, but Paris produced a frown.

"Even if what you're most passionate about is just an illusion?" he jabbed at her.

"Have you heard about this thing called the *Internet?*" she countered.

"I have heard of it. But I have not tried it," he snapped back.

Father Michael stood back as the two shot arrows at each other with their eyes.

"So tell us, why are you really here? Looking to profit from your grandmother's passing?" Paris scowled. Zoe's face fell. She looked stung.

"Paris, Zoe is a guest in our home," Father Michael nudged his son to drink his coffee, practically telling him to change the subject. "You must forgive my son. We do not get many visitors on the island. Let alone young people… *of* … the female persuasion."

"My bad, as well. I know I sound sarcastic sometimes, but you see, that's just Yiayia in me."

They sipped their coffee and avoided eye contact, both staring off into empty space. It felt like an eternity before Zoe focused her eyes again. This time they fell on a picture frame propped up on a desk against the wall separating the kitchen and the living quarters. It was of a young, beautiful woman holding a little boy in her arms as they both posed in front of Saint Peter's clock tower. There were scaffold-ings, not as high as today, but the clock still displayed the exact same hour that's been frozen in time, a mere few minutes before twelve.

"Is that Paris' mom?" she asked.

Father Michael turned, reached over and brought the frame to the table. Zoe studied the photograph with great joy.

"Yes," confirmed the priest. "My lovely wife, Catherine. She was a wonderful lady, a true friend and an incredible mother."

"Was it *love*... if I may ask?" she questioned with fervor.

"Well, it was an arranged marriage... was before I was ordained. But yes, at the end, there was a lot of love. Real love. Real crazy love," He grinned like never before.

Zoe noticed Paris lowering his head, feeling uncomfortable with the conversation. She raised her cup of coffee.

"To Catherine! To her memory!"

They toasted with their coffee cups. Paris' smile returned, but just a touch. Father Michael got up once more, tapping his finger up against his forehead.

"How absent-minded of me, I made orange cake. Just a moment," he said and walked out of the room.

"I hope I can manage one more bite," she cracked at Paris.

"Be brave, I will carry you home if necessary," he joked, much to her relief.

Maria's villa was just outside town, but they were in no hurry to get there. He even suggested a longer route through more picturesque streets, the village mostly immersed in shadows. Street lamps were sparse and most window shutters were closed, offering no signs of life. Fragrant tree branches reached over garden walls, adding to their already woozy senses. The star-studded sky danced majestically over their heads. She kept pace with him, occasionally holding onto his arm when crossing dips in the road. She was totally grateful for the poor maintenance of the cobblestones at their feet.

"Thank you for walking me home. How do you even know where you're going? I can't see a thing."

"Just look up to the moon and the stars. They'll guide you," he said, taking her hand in his and raising it toward the sky.

"Venus is the brightest star to the west. And Saturn is to the south. See...? There, and there!"

She couldn't really concentrate. She hung on his every word, believed anything he said and somehow she had faith. Come to think of it, she had never felt like this before; inebriated, mesmerized, disoriented. She was out of her comfort zone, yet she felt safe. Zoe had seen a lot in her life especially living in New York City. But her present moment was unlike anything she had ever experienced. There was no other place she would rather be right now, even if it was scary and pitch black.

"We need to head east to Grandma's house," he said. "So split the two and walk the opposite direction. This way."

"That's easy enough! You'd figure this would be in my DNA..." she remarked, excitedly.

"If all fails next time, just pretend you're an ancient living on this island 3,000 years ago. Make-believe you're Theseus and I'm the Minotaur, and you're searching for me in the labyrinth..."

"Haaa! My mom woulda loved you."

"Of course, she would have!"

That was an odd, cocky thing to say, she thought, and shot him a look. He raised his arms above his head, making fake horns, and began stomping his feet like a bull.

"Would your mom have surrendered to the Minotaur? R-RRR!" he snarled, circling her.

"Oh no, help! Help!" she played along by running away and shrieking. Paris chased her through the dark and treacherous pathways. The moon's milky glow provided them with much-needed light.

Just as they turned a corner, Zoe realized that they had arrived at the villa. She halted, almost disappointed, when to her surprise Paris concluded the chase by grabbing and squeezing her from behind and in the process sweeping her off her feet. She yelped like a little girl. And when he let her down, they both burst out laughing, grappling with each other's arms. She gave no thought to it. She leaned in and met her lips with his. To her shock, he scooted back as if hit by a bolt of electricity. He looked up to the sky as if searching for a message from the heavens. Be it from Jesus or even Zeus; he was looking for any answer. Suddenly, a thick cloud of awkwardness engulfed them yet again.

"I'm sorry," she uttered, dazed.

"No, I'm sorry," he replied, looking down.

She backed up to the front door when he stopped her.

"Zoe," he stirred up. "I want to tell you something…"

She hesitated at first, but was struck by the sincerity in his eyes. She took a small step closer to him. He seemed to be struggling with himself, trying so hard to let his words out.

"I think my mother died because of me."

"What do you mean?"

"What I meant to say… I *killed* my mom."

She was speechless and all she could see was the sky's stars reflecting inside his eyes.

"I started working on the church's clock from the time I was a young boy. I don't know what drove me to it, but I did. I was obsessed, as if the universe compelled me to… Day after day, night after night, I worked hard at fixing it. Other watchmakers from across Europe even came to the island, set up shop and tried, but they all failed. Then one day, I was late for lunch and my mom went looking for me.

For some reason, that day I chose to go out and play with the neighborhood kids—first time in years. Even today I still don't know why I did... Be that as it may, my mom went up the scaffolding to find me and that's when it happened. She mis-stepped on a ledge and fell. We found her hours later, but it was too late..."

Zoe hugged him hard, resting her head on his chest, hearing the beats of his heart.

"Oh my, that's horrible! But it doesn't mean it was your fault—"

"I blame myself. Had I not gone out to play that day, my mom would still be alive."

"You can't say that for sure. You were just being a kid. No reason for you to carry this guilt for so many years..."

"I feel guilty for my dad, too. He's the only reason why I stay on the island."

"You're a better man than most. Loyalty is hard to come by."

She released her hold and looked him in the eyes.

"Would you like to come in for a tea or something?"

"Thank you. Perhaps another night?"

She nodded.

"We have that in common," she tried changing tack.

"What's that?" he wondered, confused.

"Dead moms."

Bewildered by her off-color attempt at humor, Paris shook his head and looked away. After a few beats, he turned and split without saying a word. Flummoxed, Zoe watched him walk into the night. She stayed outside her door until all traces of his shadow and footsteps had faded.

She inhaled the aromatic sea breeze and let the silence of Petra soothe her ears. Her hand felt the watch on her left wrist as a spark of thought shot through her drunken mind.

"Pethi mou!" she exclaimed.

She pictured her Grandma Maria taking the watch off her wrist and passing it to her. When did Yiayia have that inscription made? Before she could ruminate on that, she heard a distinct shuffle within earshot. There was someone surely afoot on the cobblestones nearby, shifting about, then stopping. She shot her head around and glanced the darkness that surrounded her. The hair on her nape stood up straight. The front area of Maria's villa was still and quiet, but Zoe was certain that she was being watched. After a dozen seconds, she let it go and entered the villa. She was spooked and despite the island's motto, she had already made the decision to fix a new lock on her door in the morning. "Manos must sell door locks at his store, right?" she asked herself, convinced.

TEN

PARIS

1949

They sat on a park bench at Pont Notre-Dame, basking under the Parisian sun with their eyes closed. Though it was a poor life with hard work to make ends meet, they felt completely free. Mainland Europe was a magical place even after emerging from a brutal war. Immense healing was being had across the Continent and Paris was the place to be.

Their first stop after sailing from Petra was Italy where they sojourned in Rome for a few months, lodging with an old and trusted friend from Stephan's university days. From there, they secured legitimate Dutch identity papers for Stephan as one of his grandparents traced their ancestry back to Rotterdam. They could have easily gone to seek refuge with Stephan's family in Germany, but Maria and Stephan decided The Rhineland was not the place for them. Letters from his brother in Berlin spoke of a country in ruins.

From Italy, they took a boat to Marseilles before

traversing into the heart of The Republic. Despite wearing Greek working class attire, Stephan's chiseled facial features always gave rise to suspicion, France not being the friendliest of places for Germans post-1945. He fortunately spoke French, Dutch and Italian fluently. By the time they arrived in the French capital, Maria was five months pregnant. The couple found cover in a modest apartment on Rue Poinsot in the 14ieme arrondissement district, and Stephan had to get creative to support his family. His knowledge of languages made it easy for him to find a supply teacher job at a nearby public school. Adjusting to a new culture wasn't always easy, but they didn't care. Maria felt like a different person, though she was no longer the wildflower he had met years ago, Stephan would repeatedly say. The time spent away from Petra was having a profound effect on her. After the baby was born, she got a job as a seamstress at a trendy fashion boutique, which exposed her to high society. A world she had never experienced her whole life while living on Petra.

They celebrated their one-year anniversary in Paris by having lunch at a tiny bistro in Montmartre and ending with a romantic stroll by the river, which ultimately lead them to the bench across from the cathedral. She squinted at the setting sun, overwhelmed by emotions, thinking that her heart would just burst. Maria *people watched* as ordinary Parisians walked past, many whose chic sense of fashion seemed to turn that bridge into a catwalk. She would point out certain women to Stephan and she would comment on how wonderful they looked despite all they had endured during the war years. And she did her best to follow their lead. Yet in all that happiness, worry tugged its cursed strings. She rested her head on his shoulder.

"I don't deserve to be happy," she stated.

"Why not?"

"I don't know. I feel Petra will catch up with us... That it will eventually claim my soul."

He kissed her forehead and lovingly took her in his arms.

"You can't help it. You're Greek. Drama runs in your veins."

She jokingly punched his chest.

"I am serious." She turned and looked at the carnation on his lapel. He had bought it from a flower stand on the Seine, much to her chagrin.

"I prefer a red rose than this carnation. It's so... peasant, so cheap," she said.

"Is our love cheap? This carnation is everything to me, because you are everything to me. It's not what the flower brings to us, but the way we feel for each other, which makes it special."

She dared not reply with words. She instead hugged him tight and closed her eyes. The bells of the cathedral rang soothingly in her ears.

They entered their apartment block as the night fell and the lights of Paris glittered around them. At the foot of the marble stairs, they heard their baby crying. It echoed hauntingly from the third floor.

"She's crying!" Maria said, alarmed. She left Stephan behind and climbed the steps two at a time. The teenage babysitter looked terrified, greeting them with fear.

"She wouldn't stop! I couldn't do a thing. I'm so sorry..." she sobbed.

Stephan paused at the doorframe and observed Maria cuddling their infant daughter. Their little girl cried what felt like forever.

ELEVEN
INTERNAL FLAME

She decided that after her morning coffee she would go for a lengthy run and take the island by storm. But first, she quickly tidied up the villa. It was a sort of "getting it ready for an open house-type cleaning". Or as Zoe called it, "make the place look like it's right out of a magazine!" She got rid of clutter, swept, cleaned up the entryway and dusted the cobwebs. Satisfied with her hasty cleaning, she grabbed a quick shower, slid on her jogging outfit and split.

Away from the village, she covered unseen corners of Petra, running through rocky inclines and prickly shrubbery. The sea breeze through the challenging paths proved invigorating. At one point, Zoe paused atop a perilous boulder lodged on the edge of cliff with a panoramic view of the entire island. It was an amazing sight to see! She hopped off the rock and as she stepped onto the surrounding trail, her feet caught a time-worn, rusty sign that was flattened to the ground. Riddled with holes, the faded writing was still visible. "Warning – Keep Out!" it said, in Greek and in German. Zoe ignored the cautioning and kept running.

She eventually came across a wide patch of flat land that had been cleared of vegetation. It was chock-full of man-made dug-out patches as far as the eye can see, looking similar to a lunar landscape. Propped in one corner was a beat-up RV trailer slumped over its flat tires. Makeshift shelters with plastic tarps flapped against the wind over the various digs. Inside one of the trenches, Zoe noticed a silhouette digging away with a small pickaxe; it was the foreign woman from Stefanos' funeral. Without missing a beat, Zoe stepped into the shallow trench. Dressed in a khaki shirt with square breast pockets, desert style shorts and work boots, the woman's strong, long blonde hair was now tied in a sensible ponytail. She painstakingly worked the pickaxe with her left hand while using a delicate brush to clear debris with her right. Protective goggles masked part of her freckly face. Zoe smiled big, as she felt the luckier in this encounter.

"Hello!" she shouted.

The woman stopped and turned to look. She didn't remove her goggles, but she did raise her hand, pointing to Zoe's side.

"Hand me that basket," she said in English. Her accent was unmistakably Northern European.

Zoe followed the woman's orders and turned to a wicker basket on the ground, which was filled with golden rocks. She picked it up and crawled under the shelter. The woman took off her goggles but kept her serious face.

"So you're the granddaughter. Zoe. As in *life*..."

"Who are you?" she shot back with her best NYC brash.

"It's about time one of you from America paid us a visit," Claudia mumbled, her face still buried in her work. Zoe didn't know how to react to her comment.

"I'm Claudia," she said, extending her hand.

They quickly shook hands. Zoe sat on the ground next to Claudia as she filled the basket with more rocks. Several delicate vial holders at Claudia's side were filled with soil samples.

"I saw you at the funeral. Did you know Stefanos?"

"I did. He was German. I'm German. Would be hard for us to miss each other on Petra."

"Stefanos was German?" Zoe wide-eyed.

"He masked his accent well when he spoke Greek. His name was Stephan Mueller."

"Stephan? *Mueller*? I don't understand... No one told me, I mean—" Zoe gasped, exasperated. "So my grandmother met him during the war?"

Claudia raised her shoulders.

"Don't know. That was before my time."

"Did he ever talk about my grandmother?"

"Not to me."

"Hmmm..." Zoe was now utterly confused.

"Best you ask the real locals. They'll tell what you need to know. I stay away from all that *business* down in the village... keep to myself. I'm just an ordinary worker toiling away..." Claudia babbled on in her own defense. Of course Zoe didn't buy it. She politely changed the subject, staring at the soil in front of Claudia's knees. It glistened a bright, deep red, almost burning her eyes.

"So beautiful," she uttered, as if hypnotized. "What are you up to here?"

"The island's rich in mineral deposits and precious metals," explained the woman, waving her hand over her work. "Since the Dark Ages, locals have avowed the elements buried under the ground attract or repel visitors to the island. Think of it as a highly charged energy field. Even The Crusaders came through here looking for the Holy Grail."

"I saw a warning sign back there…"

"The Nazis were so fascinated by Petra, they set up a research center during the War. They were looking for alternative fuels to assist their war machine after they lost the oil fields in the Middle East. It's quite fitting that *Petra* actually means rock in Greek. Your ancestors obviously knew something that we *civilized folk* still know little about…"

"Well, you've certainly done your homework… But what are you looking for?"

"I have a grant from the Department of Earth Sciences at the Geo Campus in Berlin. Like I said, Petra is considered special, and the scientific community is more than interested. I will write a book on my findings *when*… I find them. The island keeps its secrets well, but I keep the faith."

"Wouldn't you get more work done with an electric drill? Because *civilized folk* no longer live in the Dark Ages," Zoe grinned, pleased with her smart-ass joke.

"You obviously haven't lived on Petra long enough."

"Let me guess, interference with the minerals and the metals?"

Zoe produced her smartphone out of her dainty Hermes pochette belt bag and waved it at Claudia.

"Ah, you do know," said the German. "The rock was exposed during a massive earthquake years ago. Much easier to dig by hand."

Zoe got up and dusted off her tights. Claudia rose next to her.

"I hope you can stand it here long enough for us to meet again."

"I know how I look, but believe me, I love nature. This island won't repel me." She pointed to the basket. "Mind if I steal a couple of rocks? I'm a clothing designer back home, so I'm always looking for cool rocks to stone-wash my garments with…"

"Be my guest," Claudia replied, sliding the basket over to Zoe. "I heard you're selling the villa. If that's true, I'm interested in buying it."

The offer came unexpectedly, and Zoe's facial expressions made it look obvious.

"I can match the current market value… Which these days, is actually not much," added the woman. "I have a sailboat. We'll take it out tomorrow and we can talk some more."

"That'd be great!" Zoe removed a foldable handbag from her belt bag. Her mind raced as she proceeded to handpick rocks out of the basket. She coughed, wiping dust from her eyes.

"All I need is to dig up the title deed and get a signature from the mayor. Then we can talk business," she carried on.

"You're halfway there. You're on good terms with the mayor, aren't you?"

"Don't think I've met the mayor yet. It's odd come to think of it… With all the formal welcomes, you'd think I'd have by now…"

Claudia chuckled as if she heard a good joke. Zoe looked like the moron that missed the punch line. She coughed again, nearly choking from all the dust.

"Who's the mayor of Petra?"

"Paris. Father Michael's son."

Zoe's face instantly turned a shinier red than the rocks she was handling. She could almost feel the yolk running down her head.

"Well…" she mumbled and swallowed hard, her nostrils flaring. "Someone ought to have mentioned it. I mean, there was ample time… wasn't there?"

Claudia smiled and placed her hand on Zoe's shoulder who looked all sorts of confused.

"In Petra, it's all about asking the right questions."

Embarrassed, Zoe turned back to the task at hand. She finished selecting a few choice rocks, placed them in her bag, then stepped out of the shelter. She paused and turned to Claudia.

"I'll think of the *right questions* for you tomorrow. You know almost everything about Petra's past, but nothing of its more recent history. That does not compute..." Zoe commented. Between the dust and the sun shining on Zoe's eyes, she couldn't manage to see the reactions of the German woman in the shade.

With a hum in her step, Zoe decided to plot a new course for her return trip to the village. By following along the seashore, she figured she could reach the harbor in a thirty-minute walk. The port of Petra was still out of sight when she came across a settlement of houses perched on the side of a bluff to her right. Whitewashed in Dodecanesian fashion but spaced widely apart from each other, they stood silently, surrounded by shrubs. There were no souls in sight. At the back of one of the dwellings, clean garments hanging on a clothesline swayed in the breeze. The doors were shut, but she noticed a slight parting of the curtains behind a window. Someone was definitely looking at her from the darkness of the home. As she strode by, she saluted, and the curtain snapped closed without further acknowledgment. She was almost at the end of the settlement when she heard the music. It was coming from the last house, the only one with a white picket fence surrounding it. She thought that odd, as picket fences were mainly an American tradition.

She moved in closer and stopped at the gate, her gaze transfixed to the door. A tacky beaded curtain hung from the threshold, partially obscuring the interior. The music kept playing. It was some Greek song she was not familiar with. She stepped through the gate and was overwhelmed by tall green plants that smelled skunk-y to Zoe. As she slowly approached the door, she parted the sparkling beads and entered the house.

"Hello...?" she hollered.

The interior was separated in two; a small living area with a comfy ottoman, and partially visible behind an archway, a little kitchen space with a table in the middle. Aaron appeared in the archway, answering her call. He wore a light-colored robe and sandals, looking very much like a biblical character.

"Oh hello," he happily replied.

It was the first time Zoe was seeing him without his sunglasses and hat. His hair had a surprising chestnut hue, while his small eyes glistened under incredibly long eyelashes. Zoe tried to mask her surprise, feeling tongue-tied for her intrusion. She stammered.

"Oh, hi. Sorry for barging in, but I couldn't resist your beaded curtain. It was so... welcoming."

"And you are welcome," he responded, raising his voice like a singer on the radio belting out a high note. He rushed to turn down the volume of his antique record player.

"I love Marinella, don't you?" he said. "She's one of the greatest Greek singers."

She scrunched her face a little, not being entirely familiar with the name. The song sounded a lot like what her mom would listen to at home, but that was ages ago. Aaron finger gunned her with both his hands, then winked.

"I'm so glad you're here. I need your help," he said. He then disappeared into the kitchen.

Zoe waited, her eyes scanning the frames that hung on the walls. Aaron returned to the living room with a baking pan.

"I made… you know… *brownies*," he said. "And I need your impartial judgment. I mean, if you're game?"

"Oh," she answered, completely taken aback. "Yes, please!"

He shoved the tray in her face. She grabbed a brownie and bit a mouthful. As she chewed, she offered approving nods.

"Very good," she said, smacking her lips against her sticky gums.

"Great. I'll get you a doggy bag." He shuffled to the kitchen and searched through his cupboards. Zoe stood by the door observing Aaron, finishing up her unexpected treat.

"So you live here?" she remarked.

"Yes. I am one of the few and privileged guests of Petra."

"How long have you been here?"

"Oh. Many years…"

"What was the attraction? I mean, how did you hear about this place?"

He stopped and looked at her with a stare that she figured odd.

"Why? What have you heard?" he asked.

She shook her shoulders to indicate "nothing".

"Admittance to this island carries certain demands that I agreed to and signed in writing. And I'm not at liberty to say much about all that—"

"Really? For living in a… *Blue Zone*?"

Now it was his turn to scrunch his face. He found a

brown paper bag and returned to the living room. He popped a dozen brownies in, crinkled the bag, and handed it to her.

"They'll ruin my figure," she said, hoping to lighten the mood. "And my mind. Haaa!"

"Just what the doctor ordered," Aaron said, twinkling at Zoe.

She took her loot and placed it inside her foldable handbag with the rocks. She turned to leave when she stopped at a photo on the wall.

"Is this *you*? In Las Vegas?"

"Yes," he whispered, taking a humble bow.

"You were an Elvis impersonator?"

"I most definitely was."

"You were… *good*."

"Why thank you." Aaron grinned with his big white Chiclets teeth.

He walked Zoe all the way to the white picket fence where they loitered at the gate.

"Will you be staying much longer?" he asked.

"Not long. I have business back home."

"Pardon. I thought this was your home."

"Not really. My grandmother was born here."

"That's more reason than most of us have for living here…"

She didn't know how to answer that. She stretched her legs, smiled and walked away. She turned back to wave goodbye, then paced away.

"Give Petra a chance!" he yelled at her.

～

By the time Zoe reached the villa, she was inexplicably giddy. Even the sight of Sophia didn't faze her. The hawk woman was on the veranda, pacing to and fro, waiting for her. Kostas, the gravedigger, was there as well, with his head down. The man looked worn out, probably from being dragged there against his will, Zoe speculated.

"Hello, Sophia!" Zoe saluted, lending an extra chirp to her voice, mostly to annoy her.

"Where have you been? We've been here for hours," snapped the woman.

Zoe kept smiling, hoping to frustrate Sophia even more.

"I went for a stroll," she replied, innocently raising her shoulders.

Sophia nodded her head disapprovingly.

"We have important business to discuss. You were in a hurry to return to America, remember?" she reminded and pointed to the man next to her. "Kostas will buy your villa. Maybe not at once, but we can come to an arrangement for sensible payments, right? And we don't need to sign any papers or anything... We're all friends here. What do you say?" Kostas lowered his head even more and mumbled inaudible words, Sophia propelling him in Zoe's personal space trying to force him to talk.

Zoe looked at the gravedigger who seemed to wish to be anywhere but there. She glanced back at Sophia and couldn't hold it any longer, bursting into childish giggles. She just couldn't help it. Sophia and Kostas looked puzzled. Zoe was now doubled over, trying hard to contain her herself.

"What's wrong with you?" spat Sophia.

Zoe straightened her back and cackled at the hawk's face.

"Sorry, but I already have an offer. And a very good one at that," she said, lying. She had not talked sums with Claudia, but Zoe didn't care. She would not give in to Sophia's bidding. She's a New Yorker, after all! "No one pulls the wool over our eyes," Zoe proudly stated to herself.

"What! Who made you an offer? How much?" hissed Sophia, her eyes shooting daggers at Zoe.

"I can't tell you. That's confidential," Zoe answered, slurring her words. "Excuse me now, but I need to lie down. I'm exhausted. We'll talk later."

She brushed past them and shuffled toward the front door. She would have loved to observe Sophia's expression at that very moment, but resisted the urge to look back. Sophia gestured angrily at Kostas to go away. He cowered further and took off like a sprinter.

"Alright. Forget about Kostas then. I will make you an offer. How about?—"

But before Sophia could finish, Zoe slammed the door shut on the old woman's face. Sophia stood there up in arms, her eyes bulging.

❧

She carried the handbag with the rocks and brownies all the way to the master bedroom and crashed on the bed with her clothes on. She didn't care that she was covered in dust. She would shower later. She stared at the ceiling with a great big smile and reached for her handbag, drawing out the paper bag filled with Aaron's special brownies. Zoe grabbed one and began gnawing at it.

"Aaron, you naughty boy," she voiced, chuckling.

She dozed off fast and the dream that followed was more vivid than most. In it, her Grandma Maria had returned to the villa dressed in a roaring twenties costume. She waved her white-gloved hands while an adolescent Zoe watched, mesmerized. "Look what I have for you," Maria said, holding a key for the younger Zoe to see. "This is your magic key," said Maria, as her little granddaughter lifted her hands up to reach for it. Out of nowhere, an owl with wings impressively outstretched, dived at Grandma Maria's hand and clasped the key in its claws. The bird flew out of the room, with Maria laughing at the entire spectacle. "Go get it, Zoe! Go get the key!" she commanded.

Zoe shot upright in bed, gasping for air. She jumped out of bed and flew down the stairs all the way to the store-room. The stuffed owl was still there, where she had moved it when she took the phonograph out just days before. Had she noticed *it* before, but ignored *it*? She couldn't remember and didn't care. The key was there, glistening under the owl's claw. She grabbed the key, rushed back upstairs to the small office and reached for the padlock on the army footlocker, sliding in the key. It fit and it clicked open like a charm. "The gods are with me tonight," she said to herself. There were dust-covered envelopes and files carefully organized in bundles, plus other items she didn't expect to find. The most surprising was a World War II German uniform and a box of various distinguishing military insignia including numerous medals and awards.

"*Stefanos...*" she thought.

She noticed an envelope with the words "Certificat de Naissance" printed on it. She opened it and pulled out a wrinkled sheet of paper that she unfolded carefully. Her eyes fell directly to the most prominent mention up top that read: "Catherine Mueller, née 21 Mars, 1949". She speed read through the document, stopping at the handwritten additions. "Hôpital Universitaire Pitié-Salpêtrière" and "Maladie de Huntington" stood out most prominently. Before she could process it all, her eyes caught another file with a red stamp of a royal crown that read: "Kingdom of Greece". She snatched the document without hesitation, knowing fully well it was the title deed to the villa.

TWELVE
MARIA'S CHOICE

1957

"We can save her!"

He finally voiced what was simmering in his mind for days. She thought it too, even if their constant squabble was tearing them apart.

"I know it, and you know it," he added. "We must return to Petra. It's the only solution. Remember what Rita wrote to you? You do believe it, don't you...?"

Stephan was standing at the door, watching his daughter sleep. The little girl's fists were clenched and her head twitched, lost in hostile dreams. A Band-Aid on her forehead reminded them of her latest injury due to her ever-increasing tumbles.

Maria stood in the hallway arms crossed, talking to his back.

"We shall do what we can for her," she said. "But if she's meant to be taken from us, then so be it. We cannot challenge the will of the gods."

He turned to her with shocked indignation.

"How can you be so cruel?" he pained, deep from his gut.

"That place is unnatural. You and I are cursed, and it will be on the head of our little Ekaterini," asserted Maria, waving her fists. "She will not be saved there, for there is no life to be gained on Petra. I've seen it. You've seen it, too. The island will eventually kill our daughter. You have to understand this..."

"So we will let her die here because of your foolish superstitions? Our girl's suffering—"

"Foolish? You're being selfish—"

"Selfish!" he snapped back.

"You're willing to trade her suffering for an even worse fate? Your fear of losing her is clouding your judgment. You're a scientist... think!"

He grabbed her by the shoulders.

"Mein Gott, Maria. Our daughter will die!"

Tears streaked down her cheeks.

"Of course I'm afraid. But what real choice do we have...?" ached Maria.

The little girl awoke from their argument. "Mama!" she called out and Maria rushed to her side, hugging and whispering reassuring words into her ear.

Huntington disease they were informed by the doctors at Hôpital Pitié-Salpêtrière. The symptoms were clearly evident early on, but Maria and Stephan had ignored them. There was no way they could have suspected. And now they were both wrought with guilt. The one consolation was that even if they sought medical attention early on, the doctors couldn't have done anything about it no matter when Maria and Stephan brought their child in, relieving them of guilt for missing the early signs of the disease. There was no cure; only deterioration, eventually leading to a slow and painful death. Ekaterini was pulled from school when her condition began to worsen and she was now failing at most physical functions. Even a simple task like dressing herself was an epic struggle. Imagine that, the daughter of a renowned Parisian seamstress who will never wear her mom's exquisite dresses when she grows up. "The world is a cruel place sometimes," Maria would repeatedly say.

Stephan felt a need for fresh air. He paused in the kitchen, his fingers brushing the carved out notches on the doorframe; a treasured monument chronicling his young daughter's growth spurts throughout the years. The last one was recently carved on her ninth birthday. His eyes burned with grief when he exited the apartment and hurried down the stairs.

He sat on a courtyard bench and gazed at the moonlit night behind a waterfall of tears. An overgrown tree by the flowerbeds held a child's swing hanging from its thickest branch. Stephan built and installed it when his daughter was a three-year-old. Ekaterini was too big for the swing now, but she insisted on using it, still enjoying her father's spirited pushes. Sometimes his strength would elevate her to the top of the swing and she would howl with joy! Stephan kept promising to update the plaything, but he kept failing to find the time. He heard the front door squeak open, and Maria approached.

"We'll go see the doctor tomorrow," she said.

"He can't do anything for her. None of them can…"

"We will not give up on her. But not Petra. Never Petra."

"It's my fault," he said.

"What is?"

"My mother died of this, so I must have it. I am the one who passed it onto her. She is just a child…"

She leaned in and took him in her arms.

"It's not your fault… it's no one's," Maria added. "We are all just broken versions of God."

"I can't let her die," he moaned in pain.

"We will do everything we can," she said. "Please promise me this one thing; never mention Petra again."

It felt as if he took forever to answer.

"I promise," he said. But she did not believe him.

THIRTEEN
FOUNTAIN OF YOUTH

Three deafening clangs on her front door kick-started her morning. She was making herself breakfast when she hurried to answer. She unbolted her door—she was more than satisfied with her fancy new door lock she picked up at Manos' mini market a day earlier—and was surprised to see Paris holding a duffel bag.

"Good morning," he said. "I brought you some clothes."

"Well, hello to you, too," she retorted. Zoe looked puzzled, but backed up far enough to let him in. He placed the bag on the table in the stateroom; the same table they used to place Yiayia Maria's coffin on the other day.

"You've stayed longer than you expected. And I remembered the size of your luggage."

"And you noticed I've been wearing the same clothes every day... My New Yorker self is truly ashamed," she pretended, bowing her head in mock drama.

"I don't mean to offend you. These are my mother's outfits. I think she was your size. You can try them on if you like?"

She opened the bag and looked at the collection of clothes. She was totally impressed, crumpled her bottom lip and nodded her head, eyes widening.

"Embarrassed, but not offended," she said. "But to receive such a gift from the mayor of Petra himself... What will people say?"

She waited for a reaction.

"You didn't tell me you were the mayor..."

"Was it important?" he questioned, emphasizing innocence.

"Well, yeah," she stressed. "I have the deed to my Yiayia's villa and I need your signature to sell it."

"Ah ah..." he reacted, scratching his unshaven chin, his eyes wandering to the ceiling.

She puckered her face, resting her hands on her hips.

"What's wrong?" she asked.

He snapped back to reality.

"Zoe... Have you considered not selling the villa?—"

"It's none of your business what I do."

"Well, that's the thing..." He stepped closer to her, once again penetrating her soul with his sea-blue eyes.

He does this on purpose, she thought to herself.

"I understand the value you give to money and the importance of your business back in America. I urge you not to make a rash decision... something that you may later regret. After all, this is your home, and you need to weigh your priorities first and foremost."

"Are you not gonna sign the deed?" Zoe looked confused and even a bit furious.

He sighed. "I will sign it. But think about it first."

"What you're saying is, *give Petra a chance...*"

"Yes. Something like that."

"I've been getting that a lot lately. Are you all in this together?"

He rested his hands on her shoulders. "Promise me that you'll think about it."

Damn your beautiful eyes! she trilled to herself. Then nodded a 'yes'.

"And just so you know, there's a thirty-day grace period after an offer has been agreed upon. It's what I think you call in America, *sellers*—"

"Remorse," Zoe quipped, head spinning. She shook her head, didn't know what to think. "Yes, yes. But it's a lot less than a month—"

"Thirty days is the law on Petra."

He then reached into his robe pocket and produced a yellow card with Greek print and an official stamp on it.

"This is for you. Keep it on your person at all times."

"What is it?"

"A pass. All guests of Petra must carry one."

"Who's gonna check?"

"It's necessary to go by the book," he said, as he turned to leave. "Just to be safe."

He left in a hurry, leaving her perplexed. But not before she smelled the burning coffee coming from her kitchen. She threw her arms in the air in exasperation as she ran to prevent a disaster.

The thirty-five foot cutter was anchored at the end of the pier. Claudia waited for Zoe on the deck of *The Mueller*. The water was crystal-clear, the typical Greek turquoise that all sun seekers rave about. Piled up the break wall was a sea of infinite boulders; a reminder of the tectonic power that dominated this region. Claudia helped Zoe aboard and showed her to the yacht's cockpit.

"Hold this," she insisted. Zoe felt distressed as she was given the helm. Claudia skipped to the bow to haul up the anchor. The sunlight shimmered on the Aegean as they broke away from dock, sailing clear away from the island. Claudia manned the sails and turned the hull to a parallel course with the shoreline. They shared a Thermos of coffee as they enjoyed the topography. Claudia turned the rudder as Zoe guzzled a hot cup of joe.

"Wow... so beautiful," Zoe announced. "If I had all this, I'd be out in the water every day."

Zoe was thrilled to be touring a new side of the island from the vantage point of the sea. She noticed the strange combination of Petra's flora with its rocky terrain, as if they were not meant to be together. She imagined Poseidon pushing rocks from the depths to the surface and Aphrodite descending with an armful of flowers to add beauty to awe. And like the sour cherry on top of her fantasy, Zoe noticed two silhouettes on a peak clearly watching the yacht. She was almost certain—by the looks of their familiar shapes— that it was Sophia and Rita.

"And there they are, the old birds... like clockwork," remarked Claudia, who spotted them too.

Zoe turned to Claudia, surprised.

"They snoop, that's what they do. I've seen them following you," Claudia added, as she took the Thermos from Zoe. "Now you steer," she pressed, passing her the helm.

"I'm not much of a sea person," Zoe pleaded.

"I know. Don't worry."

"So tell me. What's the deal with them? Sophia and Rita..."

"Rita's harmless. But keep a distance from Sophia."

"What's her... *power*?"

121

"It isn't so much a power, as it's a lack of willingness from others to fight back. They're old people, as you've already observed."

As they circumnavigated Petra, the two women on top of the hill disappeared. Claudia raised her hand toward the sea. "Keep to the left of those yellow buoys. Steady now..."

Zoe saw the buoys bobbing up ahead.

"What are they?"

"It's the formal boundary of Petra. As a guest to the island, I have signed an agreement with the authorities not to ever cross that line. The current is a bit tricky out here..."

Zoe applied herself to the rudder, except she found it resisting.

"It's pulling me!"

A sudden gust of wind lifted the sails, and the cutter slid uncontrollably over the buoys. Claudia jumped, screamed at the top of her lungs, and grabbed the tiller.

"Help me!" Claudia yelled. The two women fought against the wind and the choppy current.

They were about to hit a line of red buoys.

"*Scheiße! Scheiße!*" stammered Claudia. Zoe detected deep panic. "Help me steer the boat away from here! We must turn back!"

The wind direction changed, and the yacht tilted to the command of the rudder, one of the red buoys scraping the hull. An unearthly shriek escaped Claudia. Zoe turned to look at her, startled. The sunlight hit Zoe's eyes and she squinted in pain. Behind the sun flare, Zoe saw a Claudia that was not... *Claudia?* For a mere moment, the German woman looked pained and aged, her face cut with the lines of time with half-blind, glazed eyes and yellow teeth. The yacht veered and shifted balance, throwing Zoe to her knees. Claudia held tight and steered the vessel toward the island, pointing it directly to the shore.

"There's a good spot. We'll have the beach to ourselves."

Zoe stood up and took hold of the rail enclosing the cockpit. She glanced at Claudia, who now *looked* to be normal again.

"Are you alright?"

"Yes, I'm okay," replied Claudia, smiling reassuringly.

"What was that all about?" Zoe asked herself, choosing not to say anything more. It must have been a hallucination, a mirage of sorts and nothing else. At least that's how she explained it to herself. There was nothing wrong with Claudia's face, as she could now plainly see. But what had brought on that strange illusion? "What's wrong with me?" she mumbled to herself.

"I'm sorry for back there," Zoe said instead.

"*Alles gut.* Wasn't your fault," Claudia reassured her.

They anchored in a secluded bay where the steep cliffs on all sides kept the narrow strip of beach out of reach, and where the sea was so translucent, the cutter seemed to float in mid-air.

"I didn't bring a bathing suit," Zoe announced, watching her shadow at the bottom of the water, mesmerized.

"What for? It's just us girls here," said Claudia, swiftly shedding her clothing in no time flat. Before Zoe could think of a comeback, the German woman was gracefully diving into the sea. Encouraged by her carefree friend, Zoe followed suit, removed her clothes and dove in after her. The water was unusually cold for late June, but incredibly invigorating. She shrieked as she resurfaced, her soul baptized, her body tingling. They took laps around the cutter, delighted by the calm and refreshing waters. Moments later, and still tingling, they laid nude on the deck of the boat, taking in the sun's rays. They felt the droplets of sea on their skin quickly turn to salt.

"I could get used to this," Zoe said. "This place makes me forget about my life back home. Like that place in the Odyssey, the… uhmmm—"

"The land of the lotus-eaters. Petra does that to you. Before you know it, you won't miss a thing."

"How long have you been away from home?"

"Too long, feels like forever. I used to go back to visit during the holidays. But this is home now."

"What about… *I mean…*" Zoe shielded the sun with her hand and turned to look at Claudia. "Seems you're one of the few young people on Petra. Not many young men around—"

"You're talking about lovers? Well, I've had my fair share—"

"On this island? Like whom?"

"You know, they may look old, but there's still fire under all that snow," Claudia rebuked. Both women burst out laughing. "Don't let their appearances fool you. I come here to sunbathe often and they know it… I bet there's a couple of them right now among those trees up there, ogling at us."

Zoe immediately reached for a towel to cover herself, her gaze studying the foliage on top of the hill. Claudia continued cackling at her expense.

"What about… Paris?" Zoe asked, her blushing concealed by her sunburned face. Claudia smiled and shook her head.

"These days, my research is my constant lover. It does

fool me sometimes, but it doesn't nag me," Claudia mused. "Tell me about your lovers back home."

"Haaa! You Germans always get straight to the point." Zoe daydreamed. "Much like you, I'm too busy with my career. Though I do date and have fun sometimes—you know—when the time permits." This comment got Claudia's goat.

"In Germany, we don't ask ourselves, *Will* I sleep with someone tonight? Instead, we ask, *Who* will I sleep with?"

Claudia's point well taken, the girls lay back, Zoe keeping the towel over her nakedness.

"Are you serious about buying my grandma's place?"

"*Absolut*. My offer is 100,000."

"I was thinking more like 500K—"

"*Nein, nein*. Too high for Petra—"

"Make me another offer."

"Let me have a think—"

"I'll give you twenty-four hours. There are others interested, you know."

Claudia humphed at Zoe's counter.

"Good luck getting the price you want—"

"You'd be surprised," Zoe teased, the two women rising on their elbows, eyeing each other.

"*Sophia*?? One of her underlings...? Now, don't bluff a bluffer," said the German. "Unless you have real offers from locals or guests of Petra, outsiders don't have the right to buy property on this island. Ask around if you don't believe me."

Zoe tried to think fast, her store in Astoria flashing in her head along with Thacker's sour face at the bank. She didn't realize that Claudia had rolled closer to her until she felt her salty lips on hers. It took seconds to register what was happening; enough time for the kiss to endure, ample time for Zoe to feel the wetness of Claudia's tongue sliding into her mouth. Zoe backed away and clutched the towel over her breasts while Claudia looked at her, questioningly.

"I'm not gay," proclaimed the German without mincing words. "But you're attractive."

"Thank you…" Zoe replied embarrassingly, though regretting it straightaway. "I mean… look, let's pretend this didn't happen, okay?"

Claudia smiled, wittingly amused.

"Sure," she said.

Zoe got up and put on her clothes. Claudia kept basking in the sun. "Your boat is called *The Mueller*. "Is that your family name?" Zoe inquired, but never got an answer.

Instead, a bullhorn blasted over their heads as a navy frigate, a fair distance away, was steaming toward Petra's harbor. Claudia stood up cursing in frustration. Though she was swearing in German, the meanings of some of the expletives didn't escape Zoe.

"What are they doing? They're here too soon!" she yelled at Zoe, as if she had an answer. "*Kommen!* We need to go to port. *Direkt!*"

The ladies raised the anchor and released the sails. Zoe had to remind Claudia that she was still naked.

By the time *The Mueller* entered the harbor, the navy frigate was already moored to the dock. What Zoe witnessed after that were images sprung only from a dystopian novel. *Crazy,* she thought. This was not the Petra she had been introduced to just days ago. Benches and tents had been erected on the pier and navy personnel in white coats and military garb were at the receiving end of the long line-up of islanders. Old women and men were queuing up a fair distance, following a routine they seemed to be very familiar with.

Claudia tied the yacht in a hurry and hightailed up the pier, as Zoe tried to keep pace with her. And when Zoe edged in closer, the situation became much clearer, yet so inexplicable to her. Women and men with graceful demeanor—people she had met on the island—were now removing their coats and shirts, completely surrendering to medical exams. Doctors and nurses used stethoscopes to listen to the islanders' hearts and lungs before being shown into the tents where they were greeted by other medical staff who hooked them up to machines. A sixty-year-old man with an officer's cap and a doctor coat was seated up front at the receiving bench, reading charts with his female colleague. He was the navy chief surgeon and he had a commanding presence evidenced by a stern face, a thick gray mustache and equally gray eyebrows. Claudia marched up with her fists clenched, completely fearless.

"What are you doing here? You were not expected for another month!" she shouted, in Greek.

"Miss Mueller…" the navy chief surgeon saluted her without losing his temper. "Command moved our schedule up. It is out of my control."

"This needs to stop! Leave these people alone already!" Claudia exasperated.

"Need I remind you, you are a guest on this island? Unless you would like your pass revoked?" he tested her, matter-of-factly. Zoe felt a chill up her spine from his icy delivery.

To her shock, Zoe spotted Rita inside one of the tents as a technician was drawing her blood. The little woman saw Zoe, too, and smiled. She raised her index finger to her lips, begging Zoe with her eyes not to cause any trouble.

"How much more blood do they need to spill?" whimpered Claudia, her shoulders hung, her fight lost.

The navy chief surgeon noticed Zoe dawdling behind Claudia.

"Who's this?"

"Maria Artemisou's granddaughter," Claudia answered.

"She needs to leave immediately!" he disproved, losing his cool.

"Your arrival was not inconspicuous, now was it?" Claudia shot back, pleased with herself.

The man signalled two navy guards who moved in and surrounded the women.

"Show me your pass," he demanded of Zoe.

Before she left the villa that morning, Zoe had debated whether she was going to carry the stupid guest pass that Paris had gifted her. As a typical New Yorker—who normally does as she pleases and answers to no one—to carry such an ID, well, it just felt silly. Still, she fumbled in her pockets and it was a good thing she produced the pass, raising it to the navy chief surgeon's eyes. He frowned.

"Get off my pier. It's off limits to guests due to official business."

The two guards escorted the two women away. Claudia was irate and paced away as Zoe ran up to catch her.

"What was that all about? What are they doing to these people?"

They stopped their hurried pace near the harbor's stores, which were completely empty. The navy guards who'd ushered the ladies away from the frigate now turned around and hurried back to their ship. Claudia studied the navy ship, narrowing her eyes, seething through her teeth.

"If the world catches wind of what's going on here,

they'd rip open the islanders, then blow up the island sky high."

Zoe remained as perplexed as ever before.

"That man called you *Mueller*..."

"What of it?"

"Ain't that Stefanos' family name, too?"

"We had similar names. That's all," she responded in a dismissive tone, then stormed off in a huff.

"But hold on a sec..." Zoe stood there not knowing what to think. Claudia was long gone now, making tracks.

Zoe desperately wanted answers, so she approached some islanders who were waiting their turn in the queue.

"What do they want from you?" Zoe asked, in some of her best Greek.

"They're jealous of our youth," uttered a man, as others burst out, laughing.

She partially understood the answer, but chose to remain clueless. Sarcasm was more evident on their faces. Despite their chirpy appearance, an exhaustion of ages lingered deep in their eyes. It reminded her of a line of children waiting to be inoculated in an African village, just like one would see on TV. They looked afraid, but they kept their composure.

Zoe was suddenly surprised to see a new person; a young woman who sat on the steps of the fishing bait shop. She had long, brown hair, wore a shirt with fancy patterns and blue jeans. She was by far the most youthful person Zoe had ever encountered on Petra. She had a suitcase by her feet, which meant she had just arrived, an identification card on a lanyard draped from her neck. She looked stunningly beautiful, if it wasn't for her red, weepy face. Her eyes were puffed and she kept blowing her nose in a tissue. Overcome with curiosity, Zoe approached her.

"Hello. Are you okay?" she asked the girl.

She looked at Zoe suspiciously and nodded her head.

"I see you have just arrived. I haven't seen you here before," Zoe added with a friendly smile.

"Neither have I... seen you here before, that is," commented the girl.

"Are you an islander?"

"I am. But I don't live here anymore. I now live on Andoriani."

"How did you get here?"

She pointed toward the frigate.

"When they have business on Petra, they also transport people, supplies, mail..."

"I'm Zoe—"

"I'm Eleni."

Eleni...? Zoe thought, then dropped the inquisition.

They shook hands.

"You don't look happy to be home, if I may say..."

"It wasn't in my plans to be here either... Look at this misery," she snivelled with trembling lips, pointing to the line of islanders.

"Do you know what's going on?" Zoe asked.

Eleni shot up to her feet, her eyes transfixed over Zoe's shoulders.

"YIAYIA!" she cried out.

Zoe turned and saw Sophia approaching with her husband Nikos in tow, Zoe's voice immediately drowning in the shudder. "Oh my God, *she's* Eleni... *betrothed* to Paris?" Zoe vocalized internally.

Zoe backed off, giving Eleni room to hug her grandparents. Seems they had been expecting her and they looked so thrilled to see their granddaughter. For Zoe, Sophia was now a new sight to see; witnessing a genuine emotion from the hawk woman for the very first time. But it didn't last long. Sophia turned to face Zoe with her usual fake smile.

"I see you have met my granddaughter, Eleni. In a few days she will marry Paris," Sophia gleamed like a pig in shit. Zoe instantly gulped like a big, fat toad; the three of them almost hearing the thick, slimy lump going down Zoe's throat.

"Yiayia, stop!" gasped Eleni, in protest.

"We must catch up; so much to say, so much to organize," continued Sophia. "But first, we must obey our duty to our country," she affirmed, pointing toward the frigate.

"What duty? What's going on here?" asked Zoe.

Sophia came closer to whisper.

"You mix too much *business* in your head, my child. And at the end, you will not get any business done. So, do as I say and hurry back to America. Or you'll end up in trouble, losing your shop, you know?"

"Sophia, let's go!" yelled Nikos, who was already on his way, his granddaughter clinging to his arm. Sophia maintained her venomous smile at Zoe, then turned to follow her family. Zoe felt numb. She watched as Sophia, Nikos and Eleni ignored the long line-up, walking ahead toward the tents as if they were VIPs. The navy personnel allowed them in without delay.

This was not how she imagined her day would go when she stepped away from her villa this morning. Feeling down and woeful, she took the path up and through the village, the same route she had taken with Yiayia's casket upon her arrival just days before. As she approached Manos' mini market, she felt the urge to run inside and get in touch with America. She wanted to hear Katie's voice, just to ask if she had her regular bagel for breakfast, or any other news regarding the boutique that day. But before she walked in,

Claudia exited the store with three 375 ml bottles of hard liquor in her arms. They stared at each other.

"I need to get drunk. Care to join?"

"Amen sister!" proclaimed Zoe.

Claudia added that she had not fully hatched down her sailboat at the pier, so Zoe followed her back down toward the harbor. But before they tried to pierce through the navy security zone, Claudia had an even better idea. They cut into a narrow street, and at the third house, she pushed the door open and entered.

"Who lives here?" Zoe asked, as they followed a corridor toward a flight of stairs.

"No one. The owners are dead," replied Claudia. "Many houses on Petra are empty."

At the top of the stairs, they reached a balcony that offered an incredible view of the entire harbor, the amphitheater of houses surrounding it, and the horizon with a shadow of Andoriani in the distance. The navy frigate, the dogged personnel, the complacent islanders, the non-stop activity in the tents, *The Mueller*... were all quite visible from here.

"My God," Zoe beamed. "Can you imagine the market value of this balcony alone?!"

Claudia laughed and placed the bottles on a table. She produced paper cups out of her pockets and unscrewed the first bottle, filling the cups.

"Manos really knows how to treat the guests of Petra. Most of it is contraband, mind you. But I won't tell if you don't... Let's start with the gin, before we move onto scotch."

"What's in the third bottle?"

"A surprise."

She passed a cup of gin to Zoe. They saluted to the sky and gulped their first shot. The ladies both gasped and coughed—Zoe relieved that she wasn't the only one. She sat on a bench while Claudia took a chair.

"A bit early for me, but..." Claudia paused as she filled their cups again. "Some *Arschlöcher* really know how to open up your thirst, don't they?"

"Who was that man? Military? Intelligence?—"

"Patrikos. Chief Surgeon of the Greek Navy. He commands a lot of power—like no surgeon I've ever met before."

They ran out of gin really fast. Claudia began fiddling with the top of the second bottle.

"Unlike most Blue Zones, this place is special, you see. After a certain age—and it's always random—many islanders stop getting old. Their cell regeneration goes on uninterrupted. And we haven't yet figured out why. So if word got out, this place would be over-run with people wanting to live here, and drug companies wanting to exploit..."

"Oh myyy... That's *why* the island's locked down by the navy. And those dates on the tombstones?!—"

"This place is beyond Blue Zone. It's almost... *supernatural*. Is it the geology? Is it the water? We still don't know."

"So that's it," deduced Zoe sitting upright, charged by the alcohol. "They're testing the islanders—"

"For years, top scientists have visited Petra to seek out its unique fountain of youth—"

"Everyone on this island is a guinea pig? Is that what you're telling me?" Excitedly, Zoe had a million questions. "And what will they do when they find the answer? Make an elixir? Bottle it, and sell it?"

"No idea. I still don't know what we're looking for."

Claudia now filled the cups with scotch. Zoe didn't quite believe her inebriated friend. She glanced over to the German woman, then to the harbor.

"But you are helping them..." she frowned, perplexed.

"My research has certain terms attached to it, yes. It's the reason I'm allowed to live here."

"And what's in it for you?"

"For me, it's all about the pure science. That's it."

Zoe gulped her drink without flinching this time.

"You're full of it. It's always about the money."

"Look it..." she downed her drink and poured herself another. "Sophia has major heart disease. Rita has been diagnosed with Alzheimer's decades ago. And Manos... well, his liver is shot to hell with all that booze! But they're still alive and for some miraculous reason their diseases have been kept at bay. Imagine the good that will come out of it, should the rest of the world benefit from my findings."

"It's a gold mine, no matter how you dress it. How about you cut me in on your deal with the navy?"

Claudia laughed.

"What do you have to offer?"

"My grandma's villa. You still want to buy it, right?"

"I do. 150K is my best offer. "

"Oh, c'mon! I'm sure Mr. Navy Chief Surgeon could sweeten the roll a little. Otherwise, who knows... Maybe news of this place will leak out to the press? After all, there are no secrets on Petra, right?"

They paused in thought, unable to engage in a stare down. The bottle of scotch was half empty, and they were too tipsy to make poker faces. Claudia refilled the cups as both women snorted with laughter.

"You got it all wrong. But I'll think about it... You'll get your final-final offer soon enough. But no more bargaining."

"I promise," Zoe replied, touching Claudia's cup with hers.

Down by the pier, aside from crowds and the tents, stood the figures of Paris and Eleni. They were facing each other, standing intimately close, and engaged in polite conversation. Zoe downed her cup of scotch, but the butterflies in her stomach had not drowned. Claudia sensed Zoe's envy and turned away. Both women looked forward to their third bottle of booze.

FOURTEEN
SEPARATE WAYS

1957

She trooped past like a woman scorned, rabid mouth and
mad eyes, pushing her way through the travellers at Gare
de l'Est. Beyond little hope, she searched all the passing
faces. Anger was burning in her gut, betrayal and abandonment tearing at her soul. If she had a soul, that is. How can
she be so full of rage and yet, feel so empty? People shot
her sudden glances, thinking she was some crazy woman
who had just escaped a mental ward. "Where's Stephan?
Where's my Ekaterini?" she mouthed in silence.

Maria had been busy with a fashion show all week
and upon her return home that day, she found an empty
apartment. She had left in a hurry that morning, enough
time to sip a hasty cup of coffee as Stephan was struggling to feed an ever-suffering Ekaterini. Tears streaked
down her face as she tried to picture their last family
moments together. They all had been a blur to Maria, as
she had fully immersed herself in her job. So the moment
she discovered an empty home, she immediately knew

what had happened, and she dropped to her knees, screaming.

She figured Stephan was a few hours ahead. At Gare de l'Est, she was told that The Express to Vienna had departed at two past noon. And she knew that Stephan and Ekaterini must be on that train; it was the most logical course for Petra. They would then continue south to Bari via Naples and finally board a ferry bound for Piraeus. From there, Petra was only a half day away. But Maria was not going to let Stephan get away with this! She would give chase, catch up to them mid-trip, or reach them in Petra if need be. But she would not allow him to tear their family apart. She leaned on a pillar on the train platform and cried in silence, her mascara scarring her cheeks.

Across from the station was an array of travel agencies. She and Stephan had visited one of them for their trip to Venice many years ago. The agency would book passage and produce all the necessary visa paperwork. She walked into the office to find all the desks occupied. She took a seat and waited her turn, overwrought with emotions. Her anger and sorrow alternated wildly by the second, which obviously played with her judgment. She wasn't level-headed, nor clear-minded. In her heart, Stephan and Ekaterini had *died*. They had left her. It was over. She was condemned as a bad person in their books and they no longer wanted her in their family. Did Stephan even love her anymore? And what did Ekaterini think? Then she thought, she will catch up to them and make him regret it.

Treasonous bastard! How dare he leave her and take her only child? When years ago, she stuck her neck out to save him? *That Nazi monster!* she roared inside.

She took a handkerchief out of her purse and dabbed her tears. She held her hand mirror to her face and cleaned her cheeks. She looked at the travellers around her, many families with children and couples excited at the prospect of their upcoming journeys. There were posters of faraway places on the wall—attractive destinations—but she was here to book a passage toward... *death*. She had sat in this very place with Stephan, feeling free and in love, as they stared at the same pictures and made plans for their future.

She covered her face with her hands and sobbed. Clients came and left, and she gave up her turn several times as she sat there, staring at the floor. Eventually, Maria got up and entered an adjoining café and took a place at the bar. She ordered a cup of coffee and sipped it slowly, letting time fly by.

She pictured her family getting further and further away from her. She knew their destination, she reasoned. So she could take her time. She left some coffee at the bottom of her cup. French coffee was nothing like Greek coffee and she had not tried this before, but she knew she had the *power* within her. Maria laid a paper napkin flat on the counter and overturned the cup. After a minute, she lifted it and leaned in to read the coffee stains left on the napkin. The gods had responded. She wasn't going to lose the freedom she had struggled so very hard to get. Ekaterini was safe and she would be for a long time, and in her heart of hearts, she knew it. Her daughter would have Stephan by her side to take care of her. Always.

Maria got up and returned to the tourist agency. There was an available desk with a grinning female clerk behind it, waiting for her to speak up. The poster above the desk featured the towering Lady Liberty at the Port of New York. She looked up to it, then sat down and greeted the sales clerk with a great big smile.

FIFTEEN

GAME OF DEEDS

Stefanos' house was now home to Dimitri. Zoe stood in the kitchen with an icy glass of white wine watching the wheelchair bound man stuffing zucchini flowers with goat cheese before passing them to Rita for deep frying. Zoe had offered to help, to contribute in any way she can, but they wouldn't hear of it. "You're a guest!" they shouted in one voice. And truthfully, Zoe couldn't imagine what she could offer; she being all thumbs in the kitchen.

Dimitri's hands worked fast as he shoved the stuffing in, twisting the petals. Rita dunked the flowers into a batter before tossing them into a blazing hot cast iron caldron out of which they emerged golden brown, aromatic and mouthwatering.

The main course, oven-roasted chicken legs and potatoes, was ready for serving, while a Greek salad had already been placed on the table outside on the porch. The deep fried zucchini flowers were the pièce de résistance, Rita stating: "One must always eat them while they're hot!"

Zoe got a kick out of watching the flawless coordination between Rita and Dimitri. It was a synchronized dance, reminding Zoe so much of her own parents; mom washing the dishes, dad drying them off. Those were moments of meditative silence for her folks, unlike these two Greeks who did everything with loud commentary. It was all gossip about so and so, and that and the other, names from the cast of Petra all performed in English for Zoe to understand.

"God bless them", she thought, grinning.

Rita sang and boogied to Greek pop songs that somehow had reached the island while Dimitri jokingly gave her a thumbs-down. He then got even with her by humming a golden oldie by Tsitsanis. And beyond all that teasing, Zoe caught glimpses of loving and lustful looks they gave each other. She smiled big, wishing to have all that one day.

The day before, Zoe had consumed more alcohol in one sitting than she had ever done before in her entire life. Yet surprisingly, she woke up without a hangover in the morning. "No one gets hangovers in Greece. I don't know what it is... Perhaps it's the effects of the sun, the clean, fresh, salty air? Maybe even the barometric pressure? Who knows? But trust me, you'll not feel a thing in the morning. This is Petra!" Claudia proclaimed, as Zoe and her staggered through the village streets, cackling like a pair of drunken college girls on Spring Break. The sun began to set as the two parted ways.

The navy frigate was already making distance with the island when all Claudia wanted to do was to crash in her yacht for the night.

As Zoe struggled uphill toward the villa, she witnessed Sophia and Nikos with their granddaughter Eleni entering their home. Zoe had no clue where the hawk woman lived, but then it struck her! Sophia lived just two doors away from Manos' mini market! Close to the very spot where a falling flowerpot nearly cracked her head open on the day of her grandma's repast. Zoe was convinced that wasn't a coincidence. Yet it made absolutely no sense. Why would Sophia wish her harm? Sure, she's not the most welcoming of people. She's possibly even a witch. Nonetheless, why would the hawk woman want to threaten her, hurt her, or conceivably even kill her?

With mad conspiracy theories spinning inside her head, Zoe ran up to Rita's, who provided her with a helping shoulder all the way home. The petite woman assisted Zoe up the stairs and even tucked her into bed.

Zoe yammered about the German uniform she had found in the army trunk, and with that lead-in, Rita obliged with a bedtime story about Maria's partisan past and her love for Captain Stephan Mueller. In it, she spoke of how the loving couple had flouted Sophia's wrath. Rita painted a picture of their youthful days on the island, paced her stories slowly and peacefully, trying to lull her best friend's sloppy-drunk granddaughter to sleep. And it worked. Zoe slipped into dreamland just after five minutes.

The air was clear and gave a view to a sea of endless blue and faraway cruise ships on their way to more popular destinations. And it was a scorcher. Even under the shade of the porch's awning it still felt stifling hot. The only thing cooling them down was the taste of frosty white wine. They were already three bottles in by now.

"Ya Mas!" they bellowed, making a toast to each other. They slurped back their drinks.

"A storm is coming," Dimitri noted, studying the sky.

"Yes. I feel it my bones," added Rita.

Zoe looked up and couldn't find a single cloud on the horizon. She grimaced, wanted so badly to challenge them. She just couldn't help herself... perhaps it was her New York brashness or the alcohol talking?

"But there's not a cloud in the sky? I mean, I've been here a week and all I see is sun and blue skies..." Zoe contended.

"Ah ah. If you would like to *see* the sun shine, you must first weather the storm," Dimitri replied, smirking, completely changing the topic. This statement puzzled her even more. She decided not to press the issue, so she left it at that.

Zoe was delighted by the colors and smells of the dishes that proved themselves equally satisfying to her palate. She smiled thoughtfully at all the attempts the island was making to woo her. The zucchini flowers were delicious, the chicken legs and potatoes simply divine, the wine quenching, her hosts comforting and the view captivated her imagination. *How could I ever leave?* she thought to herself. "Screw the bank and my business back home. I can make a life here, right?" Zoe tried to convince her responsible self. Again, perhaps it was the alcohol talking.

"I'm so sorry I never came to Petra before. Grandma tried to wipe away her past and my mom fought with her trying so desperately to cling to some sort of Greek identity... And the daughter's daughter rebelled against both of them, but ultimately sided with her Yiayia. Funny how it all comes full circle..."

"Tell us 'bout your grandpapa," asked Rita, with her broken English. "Who this man Maria marry in America?"

"All I know of my grandfather, I learned from my mother. He died when I was just an infant. My mom once visited him in the hospital when he was sick and she brought me along with her, or so I was told. She did say that he took me in his arms, and apparently that was a big source of happiness and comfort for him in his final days. His name was Robert Huff, a good, decent man, as both my mom and grandma would say on the rare occasion. He was a bit down on his luck in his twilight years, but he was a very wealthy man when he first met Yiayia. He was a real estate developer from one of those old, rich families. Legend has it that Maria met him just one month after arriving in America... She found a job as a seamstress at a high-end boutique which was owned by a Greek woman. Robert's mother had her gowns made there and she would always drag her son along during her fittings. It was the oddest thing... Maybe 'cause she was a widow at the time...

Anyway. One day, Mrs. Huff grumbled about the stitching on one of her dresses and to save face, the Greek owner had one of the seamstresses get a scolding in front of her. Well, the owner had picked the wrong seamstress—Grandma Maria—that day! Mrs. Huff never had anyone so *unrefined* lash back at her. And she got the Greek version, too! Of course, Robert instantly fell madly in love with Maria. What followed after that was indeed a Greek drama, with Mrs. Huff giving her son an ultimatum: her, or the Greek Medusa, as she called her! Of course, Robert picked Yiayia, turning his back on his inheritance. Though Robert did manage to find some success on his own, he was never quite the same. He spent most of his days just loving Maria until his death..."

Zoe paused, her mind racing in the past.

"Was Maria happy?" asked Rita, warily.

"I don't know," asked Zoe, studying the flickering light in her glass of white wine. "What is *happy*? Is it what we cling to, to make our day-by-day bearable? We talk a lot about love, but love asks us to sacrifice everything... even happiness sometimes. It's crazy."

Zoe was taken aback, surprising even herself by saying something so deep and profound. The three of them looked at each other in a moment of reflection.

"Love is CRAAAZY!" retorted Rita, with big eyes. They all burst out laughing.

"Dimitri, how did Stefanos—I mean, *Stephan*—come to be here on Petra? Did it have something to do with the war?" Zoe inquired.

Rita and Dimitri's body language morphed at the sound of *Stephan*. Zoe noticed Rita giving the man a light elbow, a sort of "careful what you say". Dimitri took a big swig of wine and wiped his lips with his sleeve, engrossed in thought.

"Stephan was a German soldier during the war, yes," Dimitri recounted, slowly, making sure to choose his words wisely. "He was mortally wounded in a battle with the Greek Resistance just as the Allied Forces were advancing. *I*... found him and... *I* nursed him back to health. Well, with the help of Rita and Maria, of course. We hid him away from the rest of the islanders at first." He smiled, looked to Rita, who returned a loving grin.

"Things were different back then, you must understand... People were out for *revenge*. But soon, they got to know and understand him. He was unlike the rest of the Nazis who only wanted blood and our women... He was a good man and I respected him. Many of us did—"

"An' das how Maria and him falls in love!" blurted Rita, wanting so badly to get it out.

"My friend was a man of little words. We became best friends from that day on. You could not hate a man like Stephan—*Stefanos*—I christened him with that name." Dimitri smiled, as he reminisced. "We would sit for hours,

144

sometimes not exchanging a single word. That man had the most expressive eyes I had ever seen and eventually, I learned to read them. I had full use of my legs back then... We were young and wild. Those were great times—"

"So what happened?! Why didn't they marry? And why did my Yiayia leave Petra for America?" Zoe demanded, wanting so desperately to know. Rita and Dimitri twisted and turned inside, cat got their tongues kind of thing. Rita took the plunge.

"Love is complicate. One want this, another want that. Who know, really. One thing sure. Maria went to America for vacation only, just to check out. And if she like't, she send for Stefanos. But Maria loss touch. She never come back, no send mail..." Rita purposefully piled on her worst English, hoping Zoe would get confused and ultimately tired of prying.

"And my poor friend waited and waited... Stefanos held out hope that his love would return one day. He was the ultimate romantic," added Dimitri, smiling mournfully.

"Yes, yes... is sad," Rita cut in. "Remember we tells you that no one step foots in villa since Maria go? Is no true. Stefanos visit place all time, fix things, take care of Maria's flowers... She loved her *gari*—"

"*GARIFALLIES*! Carnations... Humph," Zoe expressed in unison. It was an "aha!" moment for Zoe. Finally, she was getting somewhere with these darn, secretive islanders, she mulled. She was proud of herself, that was until Rita wiped a tear from her eye.

"It was heartbreakin'. It was no easy life for him," Rita snivelled. "Half people hate him. Mostly Sophia—"

"She actually ordered others to hate him," countered Dimitri. "The war's been over since forever. And we won... She makes no sense, that damn woman."

"Tell me," Zoe wanted answers. "What is this power she holds over everyone?"

"Maria know how to deal Sophia," Rita stated with great pride. "Sophia was very afraid of your Yiayia—"

"Sophia was on our backs," continued Dimitri. "Like a shadow. So if we look surrendered, it's because we're old and tired. To follow along with her bidding is the lesser trouble."

"No more talk 'bout Sophia. We keep our appetites and have more chick'in and potatoes!" Rita pronounced, walking in the house to fetch more grub.

"We must always obey the cook," Dimitri winked at Zoe. She half-smiled, looked unsatisfied, had a burning question to ask.

"Tell me, young lady. What's on your mind?"

"I have—"

"One last question. Be my guest."

"But you don't have to answer it, if you don't want to. After all, I'm in your home and I don't want to disrespect you—"

"You're wondering, how did I lose the use of my legs?" Dimitri beat her to the punch. "It was the dumbest thing, really. After a day of heavy drinking with Stefanos one hot summer afternoon, we were ravenous, so I decided to butcher a chicken for dinner. As I gave chase to the chicks, I slipped, fell back, hit my head, injuring my cerebellum. Poor Stefanos carried me all the way down to the village clinic. The doctor said I would never walk again. And as history repeats itself, Stefanos, in turn, nursed me back to health."

"Oh no, so sorry!" Zoe felt ashamed for inquiring at all. "But that's not what I wanted to ask. Actually, just forget it."

Dimitri shook his head, questioning himself. He spoke

too soon and he knew it. He wanted another chance to appease Zoe.

"Ah ah. Now I'm curious."

"Nahhh, that's all right—"

"I have nothing to hide. I'm an open book," Dimitri pondered. "You would like to know why I never married? Well, that's easy. Rita broke my heart and married another man, Joseph. So it was just Stefanos and me—the two lonely romantics living up in the hills. I guess misery did love company. But the past is well behind me now, and I'm fine with—"

"Nope. That's not it either."

Dimitri did it again. He jumped the gun and he knew it. "What's wrong with me? Must be the wine," he internalized. "Just let the young lady talk, for Pete's sake!" He was mad at himself. He gave it one last go.

"You'll be the death of me. I'm an old man, my dear. Haven't got much time left. My ticker, you know..." Dimitri laid his right hand to his heart, joking, smiling.

"Okay, okay. But I've warned you—"

"You would like to know if I can have sex—"

Cripes. The man couldn't stop yakking. He's on fire!

"No!" cracked Zoe. "I mean, I know you can because Rita's over the moon... Anything is possible in this *Blue Zone*, so nothing surprises me on Petra... I mean, on the *rock*—"

"Haaa! It's actually with the help of the *blue pill*, not the Blue Zone."

Zoe looked at him, confused.

"Viagra, my dear," howled Dimitri, nearly busting a rib.

"And there you have it folks!" exclaimed Zoe as the perfect emcee. "He'll be headlining this entire week, so please tell all your friends. And don't forget about our drink specials; 2 for 1 before sunset—"

"Or if you catch a chicken, drinks are on the house!" Dimitri blurted, chuckling hard.

Zoe clapped, swaying her head about looking for a make believe audience. "My kind of humor, sir. You're so *blue*... Bravo, I mean, don't ever change. And never stop day drinking, nor chasing chicks—you'll live forever," she added, then poured him another glass of wine.

They roared with laughter, eventually stopping to catch their breath.

"What I really wanna know is how you transferred the deed to this house so quickly? I have an interested buyer and I'm very motivated and I can't wait thirty days..."

He looked at her perplexed. "I own this house... And many others like it. I let Stefanos stay here after Maria left for America. He had no place to call home. Only Greek nationals can purchase a house on Petra," Dimitri explained. "Which means you would have to register yourself as a Greek citizen first, but that will take you months, perhaps years... Nothing ever gets done on Petra in just thirty days, unless of course you have someone on the inside—"

"Let me guess. The Mayor of Petra?" Zoe interrupted.

He nodded. She shook her head.

This story never ends, Zoe said to herself, her mind racing 100 miles per hour. "And why would Claudia make me an offer if she legally can't buy the villa? Makes no sense... makes no sense..."

Just then, Rita walked out carrying a serving plate of roast chicken legs and potatoes.

"Whaaa I miss?" Rita asked, wanting so badly to be part of the group.

"Oh nothing. We were just talking about chicks... I mean, *chickens*," Zoe bumbled. "And Blue Zones——"

"And all things blue," Dimitri followed.

"You tells her 'bout magic blue pill?" Rita deadpanned. "Is okay, no be embarrass. It make't his leg go h'up..."

Silence. The three of them stared at each other for a second or two before they cracked up with tears of childish joy! They all reached out for the chicken legs.

Her hand luggage included only one pair of jeans, and they were quite form-fitting to boot. Meaning, they were not the most respectful of garments to wear on a funeral trip. She didn't know what she was thinking when she had packed her bag. What did Katie call them, again... *slutty*? "You have the perfect bod for slutty jeans. I'm so jealous!" to be precise. "Thanks Katie," Zoe aped, as she tried the jeans in front of the mirror. They had just been delivered to "Zoe's Blue Jeans Shoppe" and the girls just loved trying on the new arrivals allowing them to stay on trend. She was so impressed by how the jeans shaped her behind. "No fear of heart attacks on Petra. No one ever dies here... Haaa!" she said to herself, chuckling.

With limited footwear options, she slipped on her runners, the speckle-colored Nikes complementing her blue jeans and her solid orange hoodie. She almost never wore lipstick, but always carried one in her make-up kit, just in case. It was a natural red color that emphasized her lips without being too showy. She checked herself out in the mirror one last time, applied some final touches, her galloping heart about ready to burst through her thorax. "What are you doing, Zoe?" she asked herself aloud, taking in a deep breath. She meditated on what could possibly go

—both wrong and right—before grabbing the property deed. She folded it nicely, slid it in her back pocket and exited the villa. Zoe was on a mission.

The late afternoon glistened over Petra. Islanders were stirring out of their siestas and having their Greek coffee. Some were already at the town square, setting up tables for tomorrow's Big Feast. June 29th was Saint Peter's day, a big occasion for the island of Petra. It was the one day of the year when the sons, daughters and grandchildren of the locals would return and partake in celebrations with their loved ones. And it was all the incentive the aged folk of Petra needed to lift their spirits, pushing the tables and chairs about, whilst singing and whistling traditional Greek songs. But some whistles changed their tune when they saw Zoe passing by, waving at them with her contagious smile. Elderly eyes lost their wrinkles as they trailed her all the way to the church clock tower. And indeed, Zoe now thought of herself as *slutty*, as she could feel the entire island examining her.

Paris was up on the scaffold, busy with his usual repairs, but he stopped the moment he saw her approaching.

She looked up and called out, "Hey, need a break...?"

Paris looked at the locals, their aerials wide open, as they observed the couple's every move.

"Well, how about it?" she asked again.

"Just a minute!" he yelled, nodding.

He smiled and descended the steps two at a time. He could not take his penetrating eyes off of her. She caught his stare, puckered her lips, and shook her hips.

"Come. I want to show you something," he said. She was following him in unfamiliar land just southwest of the village. They stopped on the side of a cliff that offered a sloping view of Petra, Zoe catching a glimpse of the pier as fishermen busily decorated their boats.

"Tomorrow they will welcome their loved ones at mid-sea and will escort them back to Petra. It's a tradition... decades old," Paris mentioned, surprising Zoe by taking her hand. "This way. This is a very special place..."

They climbed a beaten trail through jagged rock with hardy fig trees rising in-between ancient crevasses. Paris guided her as they passed through an impossible barrier, only to reach a peak over the island that took Zoe's breath away. What's more, the main attraction was not the view. It was the medieval castle that towered in front of them. Canon muzzles struck through dozens of embrasures above their heads, taking aim at the sea. Zoe was in awe. "How come I didn't notice this place earlier?" she asked herself, enthralled. It made sense that the natural slope of the cliff prevented this well-preserved treasure from being visible from the harbor.

"My God, what is this place?" she uttered to him, wanting so desperately to get answers. Paris was more than pleased by her reaction.

"Follow me. I'll show you," he smiled, still holding her hand.

Set atop the arched entrance was a grand turret made up of colorful brick. He led her through it as she looked about in a daze. Parts of the castle's original interior had fallen by marauding invaders and by the uprooting strength of the local flora over the centuries. It was mother's nature sarcastic way of saying, "I'm stronger than all of you, never forget that!" Overgrown grass and patches of poppies carpeted the entire courtyard. Underneath it all, weather-beaten stairways provided directions to the battlements.

"Well before my time, this castle was the island's main tourist attraction," Paris said, pointing to the main tower at the end of the fortifications. "Petra was settled in the 5th century BC by the Dorians. This fortress was built over the ruins of an acropolis. It was later fortified successively by the Greeks, the Romans, the Byzantines, the Knights of St. John, and the Ottomans."

She glimpsed at whatever he was motioning to, her attention focused on his face, trying to picture his chin beneath his neatly groomed beard. She imagined him in knight's armor, his strong cheekbones protruding through his helmet.

"Four hundred years ago a Pasha took residence here," he continued. "He had several wives. And when he had male visitors, he would share his wives with them all…"

"The wonders never cease!" she laughed, hanging from his arm.

"Until this day, we're still finding remnants of the Pasha's opulent lifestyle all over the island."

They climbed the broken and uneven steps with great caution. A perfect excuse she needed to cling tighter to him. They stopped at a gun hole and gazed at the incredible vista. The air was pleasant and garden-fresh. And the view of Andoriani from this lookout point was better that any other vantage point Zoe had seen. She could even make out the cruise ships docking and departing on the main island's port. It felt as if she was watching the outside world from another dimension, another point in time. Combined with the pre-evening colors, the moment weighed heavy, almost melancholic. But she didn't mind. She held his arm with her hands and she felt really safe. She looked at him and realized he was looking at her, too.

"Thank you. This is so beautiful," she whispered, unexpectedly getting choked up. "I've never been to any place like this before…"

A tear trickled down her face. Like magic, he leaned in and kissed her on the lips. She grabbed the back of his head gently, pulling him closer, making the kiss last even longer. And deeper. His hands caressed her back and with her free hand she guided his hands lower down to her waist. She felt her knees melting when his palms brushed her behind. And then, he leaped back as if stung. This time, she didn't let him go.

"I must be crazy," he uttered, out of breath.

"That helps sometimes," she said, leaning on him. He pushed on her shoulders, trying to keep her at bay.

"Zoe, you don't understand…"

In the awkward pause that followed, they both heard the flutter of paper as it tumbled to their feet. They looked down when Zoe realized the deed to the villa was pushed out of her back pocket by the tightness of her jeans.

"What is it?" Paris questioned, finding a reason to escape their intimate lock hold.

Zoe grabbed his face and made him look at her in the eyes.

"Forget that. Let's get back to kissing…"

He bent down and lifted the paper.

"It's the deed to the villa," she said regretfully.

He nodded his head, making a face.

"Was wondering what your next move was going to be—"

"Paris—"

"All these charades, so you could make me sign this piece of paper? Is this so important to you?"

"No… Yes… I mean… I don't know," she stuttered,

trying to sort out her confusion. His hardened stare was not making it any easier. He looked hurt, and she felt guilty.

"I wanted you to sign it, but I wasn't expecting this. None of it. How could I?"

Upset, he handed her the document and searched his pockets for a pen.

"If leaving this place is so important to you, then by all means. I will sign your deed so you can get your money and go back to America to make some more, if that's what matters the most to you." He raised his hands open and yelled, exasperated, "I don't have a pen with me! If you can wait until we return to the village... You will also be required to expedite your nationality, just so you know. And now I'm wondering what else you have in store for me—"

"Paris, please..."

He wasn't giving Zoe the time to redeem herself, certainly not now. He was too angry. He turned around and quickly paced out of there, leaving her alone at the battlements. Her first urge was to run after him, but a pang of stubbornness arose and took over.

"There's a storm coming! Good luck finding your way back home!" Paris yelled. Zoe looked up to the skies, and again, found no cloud in sight. She fumed, shaking her arms.

"Oh, to hell with you! And to *all of Petra!*" she shouted, but he didn't turn back as he passed through the castle's gate. She immediately felt wretched for her outburst, hoping he didn't hear it. "Fat chance," she said to herself.

❧

She took the long way back home, taking her time, ruminating. All around her, the old residents of Petra were busy dressing up their houses with flags, colorful pom-

poms and flowers. Once more, she venerated their energy and spirit as they climbed up ledges and balconies to drape the decorations. Most of them ignored Zoe as she walked by.

She felt depressed and dared wonder—if by some miracle—Manos stocked Rocky Road ice cream? "Fat chance", she thought. Nonetheless, once she saw his store-front she dived in for an illusory slice of New York. She gave Katie a call and was told their website had just launched with some promising news; orders were trickling in from members, in addition to first-time shoppers. Katie sounded as if she was getting the hang of managing the store all on her own. But on the grayer side of things, the bank refused to extend its deadline. For a moment there, Zoe thought about dropping it all and staying in Greece forever. The idea did cross her mind several times throughout the past week, but this time she was so very close to telling Katie the store was now hers. *I can see myself marrying Paris and being a priest's wife... There are worse places in the world to live than on Petra,* all crossed her mind, and a great deal more. She was bombarded by a thousand thoughts. She couldn't breathe. She felt a panic attack coming on as the phone cabin was closing in on her. Zoe quickly hung up and made a beeline for Manos. And as always, he refused to take her money.

"*In any moment of decision, the best thing you can do is the right thing, the next best thing is the wrong thing, and the worst thing you can do is nothing...* – Theodore Roosevelt," Manos stated with a satisfying smile.

"*You either master money, or, on some level, money masters you...* – Tony Robbins," countered Zoe.

Manos had no clue who Tony Robbins was. None-theless, he was impressed, felt challenged, so he decided to continue his game. He thought long and hard.

"*A good decision is based on knowledge and not on numbers...* – Plato."

"*Think like a queen. A queen is not afraid to fail. Failure is another steppingstone to greatness...* — Oprah Winfrey."

"O-*pera*-h...?" Manos shook his head, having no clue.

"You know... Just forget it," she grinned, lighting up her face.

"Take this. You'll need it for later," he added convincingly, handing her some free merchandise.

She smiled politely and left the store carrying a bottle of gin and a yellow pack of Karelia cigarettes. She immediately sparked up a smoke and sucked it back. After all, he had no ice cream.

As she approached her grandmother's villa, she saluted an older man and woman descending the twisting alleyways. They looked to be in a hurry. Zoe was struck by the dirty look they gave her as they passed on by. It was the first time she had noticed that couple. "What have I done to everyone? Why is everyone riding my ass?" she thought, flustered. That feeling increased as she stepped closer to her front door, which stood ajar. In reality, it had been kicked open. There was a dent on its lower frame and the bolt on her new lock had its casing ripped to splinters.

Zoe shuddered and felt the hair on her nape tingle. She took ahold of the gin bottle by its neck and held it like a club as she stepped into the house, battle-ready. She searched both floors, but there was no one. And there were no signs left behind by the intruders. Had someone just kicked in the door and hightailed it out of there? Perhaps it was meant as some sort of message? Zoe was already feeling unlucky, so it was easy to make these assumptions.

She sighed, as the weight of self-pity engrossed her. This day was not ending well and a cold chill blew in her heart.

"Ground control to Zoe… Try and keep it together, girl," she said aloud, needing some encouragement.

She remembered her apartment in New York had been burglarized once. "I survived that, so this was nothing," she repeated to herself. She went to the kitchen to fetch a clean glass as she unscrewed the bottle of gin with her teeth. She lit another cigarette.

It was early evening when she heard the thump on her door. She waited for a second knock, but nothing. And it wasn't just a knock; it was a real, hard, violent thump. Did she imagine it? She walked to the door, but there was no one there, though she could hear distant conversations from the other houses. As she backed away, she noticed a bundle at her feet. It looked ominous, and she couldn't make out what it was in the twilight. Zoe reached down with great caution and took it in her hands. It was a pile of letters tied together with a colorful string.

She returned to the stateroom, turned on a lamp, and drew out one of the letters from the pile, reading the address. The recipient was Stephan Mueller, with his house number in Petra. All the envelopes had the same address. She flipped them over to read the name of the sender. It was the same New York City address on all of them. These were letters written by Maria.

SIXTEEN

THE PROPHECY

1988

Sophia was honestly scared. She was a hardened woman and few things elicited fear in her, having lived through World War II, and later, the Greek Civil War, which included forced starvations. But here, at this very moment, the other woman who sat across from Sophia at her kitchen table holding the smeared coffee cup terrified Sophia like no one before.

"You cursed pure love and you chained us all under your spell. It had nothing to do with them. Your ego and vindictiveness no longer holds power. You are nothing," said the strange woman with great composure.

"How dare you talk to me that way! I will not allow it!" Sophia shouted at the top of her lungs, the dishes on the racks trembling.

The woman slid her fingers across the rim of the coffee cup.

"Have I ever lied to you? Have I ever been wrong?"

Sophia lowered her eyes.

"One day Maria will return. And on that very day, a new love will be born. And the spell will finally be broken," continued the woman with a devilish smile.

"NO!" cried Sophia. "You are mistaken, Ekaterini! You will see! I will not allow it!"

"It is written," said the woman. She let the coffee cup down, got up, and left the room.

Sophia shrieked and yanked the tablecloth in such a rage, it sent the coffee cup smashing into the wall and shattering into a pile of pieces that settled at her feet. The gods had spoken. And that would have been the narrative for most people. But for Sophia, being who she was, her vindictiveness grew even bigger and stronger.

SEVENTEEN
WRITTEN IN STONE

I don't know what to say. I've been robbed of my soul. How can I truly express my anguish on a piece of paper? Will you read this letter? Have you read any of my letters? Ever since I started writing to you, I've pictured you burning all my unanswered letters, but I've kept writing, nevertheless.

You can imagine my shock, when after all these years to finally receive a letter from you. I knew from the moment I saw your name on the envelope that this was not going to be good news. I couldn't open the letter for days. And when I finally did, my world came crashing down. Through my heartache and tears, my first reaction was to curse your very existence. Was that your way of intentionally inflicting revenge on me? How could I even enjoy the belated news that I also had a grandson? Perhaps I deserve your cruelty. If those were indeed my Ekaterini's last words that she had addressed to me, then I understand, Stephan. I would like you to know that I understand now. How could I blame you when you did your best for our little girl?

Our beloved daughter is dead... But not because of the island. She's dead because I was not there to save her. When we are young, we think we can control our destiny... How arrogant of us. For

*time always has the final word. It flows without end and it can
also stand still, should we choose. The one thing it does not do is go
back to remedy our mistakes.*

*This is my last letter to you, my Stephan, my love. I don't
think I have anything more to say. I have never stopped loving you.
And I have never loved anyone else like I did you. You did not fail
me... I failed you. I have lived with my choices and their conse-
quences. If anything, our Ekaterini's boy is our last hope. As for
me, I have given my trust to time, for it always wins, until the day
it will reunite us all, together again.*

After reading this last letter, Zoe stopped wiping away her
tears. Maria's letters, all written in English for some reason,
were sprawled across the dining table. It was a one-way
correspondence that had started in 1963 and ended in
1988. She began writing to Stefanos six years into her
marriage with Robert Huff. Her early writings were mostly
expressions of a masked regret, which became more
apparent as the letters continued. Maria's references to her
married life were matter-of-fact and always brief. She
mostly reminisced about her love for Stefanos and persis-
tently asked questions about their daughter, Ekaterini. All
the envelopes were unopened and sealed, except for the last
one. For some reason, Stefanos had read that very letter.

Dawn's early light crept through the shutters, stinging
Zoe's sleepless eyes. She looked to her busted front door
and lock and didn't care. She was balancing on a tightrope
of feelings, and she feared that any emotional outburst
would send her tumbling. "Oh Yiayia, what did you do?"
she mumbled, yet fully understood that if it wasn't for her
grandma, she would not be here, alive on this planet and in
this villa. Yiayia had survived Ekaterini's absence with the
help of new daughter; Zoe's mom... Patra.

Zoe was now overcome with tears and felt the sudden

need to pull herself together. She ran out of the villa, leaving the door as she had found it. She walked the empty streets, not paying attention to the house fronts that were pleasantly decorated for today's Big Feast. By the time she reached the cemetery, the sun was shining bright. There was a little drummer in Zoe's head, thumping to her heartbeat like a bass drummer of a parade, yet it refused to take a coherent form. She so badly wanted to scream out the words hanging off the tip of her tongue, but she couldn't. There was not a soul in sight.

The rusty gate of the cemetery screeched wide open with her push. Zoe was a woman possessed, ripping weeds and vines off the headstones, searching for something in the inscriptions without really knowing what she was looking for. The names of the deceased may have sounded unfamiliar to her, but the dates were truly unforgettable. She couldn't believe her eyes! The youngest person to ever die on Petra in the last half-century was aged one hundred and two. In fact, some islanders had even reached the age of a hundred and fifty and higher! "*Their secrets are written in stone,*" were Stefanos' last words to her. Perhaps even his final words on earth?

Zoe paused for a moment to reflect, taking in a long, healing breath. She then turned her attention to the first row of headstones where the two new graves of Maria's and Stefanos' both shined a golden hue under the sunlight. With her heart charging, she looked to the grave next to theirs. It too was well-groomed, its white marble washed, its candlelight aflame with a bunch of fresh flowers in a pot. It read: "Catherine Artemisou-Mueller, 1949 – 1988".

"Catherine…? *Ekaterini*?? Oh my God!" Zoe screamed.

She sprang to her feet and began stirring in circles. Her stomach was doing cartwheels all the way up to her throat.

"Whoa!" she yelped, with an image of Yiayia in her

head. "This is too Greek! I mean… it's just sooo Greek!" She laughed hysterically.

The taste of his lips returned to her mouth and they felt sweet once more. She slid her face in her hands and rapidly did the calculations. All they shared was a common Yiayia. "So Stefanos is *not* my granddad. Phew!" Zoe reassured herself. "But what does that make us…? Half-cousins? Shut up!" she replied to her own jumbled mind.

Zoe took in a lungful and reached out to Catherine's headstone with her right hand. She rubbed the surface, touching the etchings, running her fingertips over her name.

"Now why did you take your own life…?" she whispered to the dead.

She left the cemetery behind her and stood at the edge of the sea, hoping for some clarity in the morning breeze. The day greeted her with the blast of a hundred horns. The festivities for Saint Peter's Day had just got under way. The navy frigate entered the harbor, escorted by numerous fishing boats jammed with jubilant islanders. Women, children and men on the deck of the ship waved colorful scarves and handkerchiefs to their relatives on the boats, their joyous shrieks overwhelmed by the tooting horns. Many boats burned flares raising a celebratory smoke over the gulf.

She took the road to the church, feeling invisible for the first time since she arrived to Petra. No one seemed to notice her, as old women and men alike, dressed in their elegant dresses and finest suits rushed to reach the pier before the big ship docked. At the town square, the horse-drawn carriage delivered barrels of wine. The tables and

THE ISLAND OF ZOE

chairs were arranged in orderly rows and facing numerous half-cut steel drums propped open with burning fires. About a dozen elderly men busied themselves by chopping goat meat and vegetables for the stew that would soon feed all the celebrants. Zoe passed the clock tower where she found the workshop's door was locked, so she continued to Father Michael's home. The front door stood open. She paused before she knocked on the doorframe. There was no response. She braved a few steps in.

"Hellooo...!" she called out.

Father Michael was in the living room, adjusting his priestly attire in front of a mirror. He spotted Zoe behind his reflection and smiled warmly.

"Good morning, my child. Come in!" he greeted.

She felt awkward as she approached. He turned to face her.

"How are you on this glorious day?" he asked.

"I'm fine, Father. Is... Paris home?"

She detected a hint of discomfort in him, as well.

"He's down at the pier... with Eleni."

"Oh, then could I—"

They heard footsteps approaching outside the front door. Before Zoe could turn to look, Father Michael grabbed her by the shoulders and pushed her into the adjoining room. As he backed away to the living room, he signalled her to keep still and be quiet. He closed the door, but it creaked open on its own, allowing a narrow view for Zoe to see.

Sophia and Nikos entered Father Michael's home, the hawk woman looking and behaving like her bitter self, although Zoe couldn't make out what exactly was being said. She cursed herself for never fully learning to speak Greek. Sophia sounded bossy, stressing her every point with big hand gestures, whatever that was. Father Michael was on the defensive, Zoe never noticing him so overwhelmed before. Sophia mentioned the names of Paris and Eleni and also heard her own name, as well.

Her instinct was urging her to burst into the living room and openly confront the hawk woman, but then she considered Father Michael's position; he had concealed her in this room and she wondered why the priest did that? The argument in the living room went back and forth with Sophia on top and Father Michael losing ground. In one hissy burst, Sophia even shouted the names of Paris and Zoe together. With great effort, Zoe managed to remain calm. Nikos seemingly tried to contain his wife, but to no avail. And when he brought up Maria's name, Sophia lashed out. Eventually he bellowed, "God help us!" in Greek, which Zoe understood, followed by a verse he recited, in English:

"*Behold, this third time I am ready to come to you, and I will not burden you. For I seek not what is yours, but you. For the children ought not to treasure up for the parents, but the parents for the children.*"

In return, Sophia proclaimed in English. "Pray on this. My granddaughter will help us populate the island with young Greek blood again, and more of our people will return and the school will open up. And Zoe and her kind will be gone forever. Mark my words!"

With that, the hawk woman exited the house, dragging Nikos along. After a brief moment, Zoe stepped out of her hiding place and stood in front of the priest. Father Michael wiped the sweat from his forehead with a hand-kerchief.

"Sorry about that. Marriage arrangements…" he affirmed, fake smiling.

"I heard my name. Am I being considered as a brides-maid?" she joked.

He didn't get her sarcasm, nor did she care to explain.

"I am sorry, too, Father. We'll talk later," she said, dashing out.

~

As she walked down to the port, the islanders were climbing the road back into the village, their faces beaming in the company of their beloved sons and daughters and grandchildren. It was a festive parade of chatter and laughter. Children squealed and ran about, almost bumping Zoe up against a wall. She tried to smile at some of the families, but mostly, she felt sad, felt too much like an outsider. The bedlam she met at the port was not all smiles and confetti. The navy was also there, double-checking the papers of all those disembarking with the navy chief surgeon overseeing the outflow of passengers. The light of Saint Peter's Day was amiss in his cold facial features. Families, priests and dignitaries stepped onto the pier, but not a single tourist. A group of musicians crossed the drop bridge carrying guitars, bouzoukia, clarinets, fiddles and percussion instruments. Even Mr. Kanakis from Andoriani was among the visiting public officials. He recognized Zoe and stopped her in the mob.

"Miss Zoe!" he cried out. "I didn't expect you'd be still here."

"I have some business to take care before I leave—"

"Oh lovely! How fortunate for you to witness the Big Feast," he added, giving her a warm smile.

Before she could agree, a commotion broke out on the deck of the ship. The entire pier watched as the navy guards manhandled an older couple whose papers were apparently not in order. By the way they were dressed, Zoe could have easily mistaken them for dignitaries, which apparently they were not. "Xeni!" (*Outsiders!*), someone shouted in Greek. Non-locals, trying to infiltrate Petra, Zoe thought. The crowd suddenly fell quiet, the desperate cries of the older couple and unfolding drama clearly audible to all.

"Please, my wife doesn't have much time to live!" the old man yelled desperately to the guards who were pulling him away from the drop bridge. He produced a stack of money from his breast pocket and waved it over his head. "Please, take it! I have plenty more!"

The guards ignored his plea, forcing the sobbing foreign couple back onto the ship. Right then, a push and a shove scattered the bills onto the deck of the pier.

"Please, have mercy on us!" continued the old man. "Don't you have a mother? How can you do this to us?"

The couple was now hauled out of sight. The festival-goers, slightly dismayed, immediately forgot what had just happened and returned to their business at hand. Order was quickly restored and the festive hullabaloo returned.

"Sorry, you had to see that," Mr. Kanakis apologized. "What an unfortunate affair..."

"Seems like no one cares," Zoe appended, indicating to the crowd. She then shot the navy chief surgeon a dirty look. He returned her look of contempt, then turned away.

"They're used to it," Mr. Kanakis answered. "Sadly, this happens often." The man felt awkward and sought a way out. "Ahhh, I see the mayor! Excuse me, Miss Zoe..."

"The mayor? Where is he!" she yelled over the commotion, surprising even the official. Zoe popped her head about and spotted Paris in his finest vestment, shaking hands with some officials. She pushed through the multitudes of people toward him, leaving Mr. Kanakis dumbfounded but relieved to part ways.

Zoe reached Paris as he was showing his guests the way

to the Feast. He saw her coming and politely paused to wait for her. He produced a courteous smile, making her wonder if that was worse.

"Good morning," he said to her. "I still don't have a pen on me. I promise that after the celebration—"

She couldn't believe that was the first thing he said to her.

"Shut up."

Zoe wanted to say something else, something so important, but the words refused to come out. The picture of a young boy crying over his dead mother flashed in her eyes. His eyes stared at her, bluer than ever before and she felt her legs buckling. She stood there, mouth open, mute like a complete idiot.

"What?" he tested her, waiting, perplexed.

He already knew. He knew all the secrets she had discovered by herself this morning. And now she was afraid to say them aloud, else she would end up bawling in front of everyone. She suddenly grabbed his arm, as if seeking support.

"Do you love her?" she asked, her throat burning.

His puzzled stare continued.

"Do you love Eleni?" she pressed.

It was his turn to struggle to find the right words, but it was just too much for him to handle. His silence lasted what felt like a lifetime.

"I hope you'll be happy together," she pronounced. Zoe then turned around, diving into the solace of the crowds.

She sat on the steps of the port's bakery and sulked as the cheery crowd disappeared into the village. She just wanted to crawl up the cobblestones all the way to her bed and wait out this day in self-pity. Then a shadow fell on her, catching her attention. It took a while to register it was Aaron. He was sporting a full-traditional islander costume with impressive deep blue breeches. She was surprised at how easily that made her smile.

"Aaron, what are you wearing?" she questioned, giggling.

"It's a day of celebration, is it not? In honor of my hosts, today I'm as Greek as can be. What are you doing sitting here all alone? The feast is up there..." Aaron motioned.

"I wasn't planning on going."

"And miss the free food and wine? Now that's just foolish... Ma'am, if you could do me the honor…" he asked, extending his bent elbow to her.

She instantly felt better. She was being overly dramatic, and she knew it. Her heart was broken, and other than her villa's front door, there was really no other damage. *It was just an innocent kiss*, she thought. *Stop it, Zoe!* she screamed to herself.

Zoe took Aaron's arm and the two of them followed the latecomers up to the Big Feast.

When they reached the town square, they noticed the tables were mostly empty. The crowd was squeezed into the church observing the Saint Peter Day service. Father Michael's chanting was clearly audible to the few worshipers outside who couldn't get in. Zoe and Aaron sat at a table on the edge of the square to wait out the service. Soon, the crowd spilled out into the square and filled the tables.

Aaron, like a considerate date, ran back and forth to the

service area to provide stew and wine for the both of them, but mostly wine.

Sleepy as Zoe was, she felt her senses were deeply on edge. The musicians were propped under a huge fig tree near the church, which provided shade from the burning sun. They played cheerful folk music while the local women took turns singing popular songs. A collection of guests and locals, young and old, danced together in traditional circular form at the center of the square.

~

Paris and Father Michael sat at the long table with other dignitaries, including the Bishop and the Mayor of Andoriani. Father Michael took care of pleasantries while Paris downed wine glass after wine glass.

"Slow down, son. The entire archipelago is watching," Father Michael murmured, as he smiled and scanned the crowd.

"With all due respect, *Father*, do not tell me what to do. Certainly not at the eleventh hour," Paris seethed back.

"I trusted this is what you wanted—"

"On the contrary. This is what Sophia and the others have wanted for me. And you've never stood up to them. They destroyed Maria, Stefanos, mother... And now I'm next. But I'm fine with the lot I've been given. I just ask God to forgive you all."

Paris guzzled back a glass of wine, then poured himself another. A tinge embarrassed, Father Michael shot nervous glances around the church square to see who was watching.

~

All of Petra's motley cast of characters were present and accounted for, as Zoe observed. There was even a table for the foreign guests of Petra. The Manos mini market trio; the imaginary British Prime Minister, the Hollywood actor lookalike, and the *other one* were there. Plus some foreigners Zoe had never seen before.

Manos sat a few tables down enjoying time with his family, sandwiched between his son and his grandson, looking elated. Zoe was also surprised to see how *old* Manos' son looked as compared to him. Very odd, she thought. She then moved on to Rita and Dimitri who shared the same table with their loved ones, all of whom looked unfamiliar to Zoe. Sophia and Nikos sat with what looked to be their daughter and her husband. Curiously, their granddaughter Eleni didn't seem all that happy. Zoe then glanced over to the head table and noticed Paris slightly inebriated. She stared long and hard, as though she was meditating. Her mind wandered as she tried to slow her breathing.

Aaron raised his wine and proposed a toast. They clinked glasses and smirked at each other. Zoe didn't care much for the wine's aftertaste, but she kept drinking, none-theless.

"Aren't you going to dance?" she asked Aaron.

"Oh, I will! But this folksy stuff isn't my cup of tea. I'll wait for the music to shift, you see. Once their nostalgia wears off and the wine kicks in, they'll get their tunes closer to my heart. I want to dance a zeibekiko... Now that's a dance! Greek. Manly. A contained power of explosive expression. No fancy moves; a brooding dance, not a happy one. A zeibekiko is danced within a two-by-two perimeter around the dancer. And you know why...?"

"I haven't a clue—"

"To resemble and to remind us of a holding cell in a

police station. That's where the zeibekiko was born. It's a source of pride for every palikari (*lad*) that found himself imprisoned by *The Man*, and opposed his resistance by dancing... even in prison."

Zoe smiled as she watched Aaron guzzling his wine, looking eagerly at the dancers in the town square.

"Do you miss it? The show...? You know, impersonating Elvis?" she asked.

"Nahhh. That's in the past," he said, without looking at her.

She noticed Claudia standing in front of the table of the foreigners and chatting intensely with the "ex-female Prime Minister". Both of them turned to look at Zoe who felt suddenly exposed to their attention. Claudia smiled and left her company, walking to Zoe's table, dragging a chair with her. She sat across from Zoe.

"I came by the villa this morning looking for you. What happened to your door?—"

"They didn't like my lock—"

"I'm not surprised. Didn't you get the memo? No locked doors on the island."

Zoe couldn't maintain a smile.

"I come with an offer of 175,000 Euros. It's my final-final offer. I take it broken door and all. Do we have a deal?" Claudia beamed. Zoe looked displeased.

"Thank you for the offer. But I have a question..." Zoe stated, all business.

"I'm listening."

"I was told that guests of the island cannot purchase property. So how would that work?"

Claudia lurched hard, suddenly losing her ability to speak. As she searched for her words, Zoe turned to look at Paris.

Her heart sank. Paris looked glazed over from sweat

and alcohol. Zoe looked to Rita and Dimitri for their support, but they were too involved with themselves and their families, happily smiling. She then noticed Sophia giving Rita and Dimitri disapproving squints. Zoe felt so very alone.

A week ago, none of this was even a glimmer in her imagination. A week ago she was unpacking a large delivery of blue jeans summer shorts in her store. Maybe all of this was just a dream and it was about time for her to finally wake up. This illusory offer for the villa was a good one. It could prove to be a real lifesaver, if it were real, of course. Zoe imagined Thacker's expression as she shoved her bank check to his face. Yet "I'll think about it" was what she heard herself saying.

"You know, selling your grandma's home will not make you happy in the end..." Claudia interrupted Zoe's thoughts, surprising her.

"Pearls of wisdom," mumbled Aaron, keeping his eyes on the festivities.

"Though I do not wish to lose the sale," Claudia continued. "I just felt the need to say that."

"I want 175K in cash. Within a week or no deal. Can you swing that?" Zoe countered, poker-faced. Claudia and Aaron glimpsed at each other, completely speechless.

Just then, a folksy song concluded and everyone applauded the musicians and the dancers. Festival-goers looked about waiting for the next song to begin, giving Paris the perfect cue to change the pace and tone of the party, or at least that's what he thought. He shot upright, sending his chair to the ground. As he walked around the table, Father Michael tried to reach out for him, unsuccess-fully. Paris paused in front of the musicians and yelled out his order.

"A ZEIBEKIKO!"

The musicians hit their chords and the crowd began to clap in rhythm, encouraging and leading Paris. He stomped his feet, bent his back and swayed his arms. Zoe turned to look at Aaron.

"There you go! Get up and join him," Zoe encouraged.

"What? No way... The Zeibekiko is a solo dance. If I join in, I will offend his manhood. Much blood has been shed by this very insult. Study your history, my dear," Aaron replied.

The crowd clapped around Paris as he twisted and turned, never abandoning his spot, those closely gathered around him delighting in the artistry of his dance. Aaron and Claudia got up to cheer him on. Even Zoe started clapping, absorbed by his intoxicating and pained facial features, when of a sudden she stopped, feeling her heart racing. She downed her glass of wine in a single gulp and to her own surprise, she leaped to her feet. Zoe approached Paris with her arms outstretched, then paused in front of him at breathing distance. She had no clue how to dance the zeibekiko, but she didn't care. She jumped right in with all the courage she could muster. The applause and cacophony stopped, and a collective gasp erupted across the town square. The musicians lowered their instruments. Paris froze and stood there looking at her, their eyes locked.

"Figai apo ki! (*Get lost!*)," an anonymous woman shouted out, furiously. Zoe did not turn to look. Perhaps it was Sophia? Perhaps it was someone else? She didn't care. This here—whatever it was—was time standing... *still*. For her, it was the Paris and Zoe dance.

"What are you doing?" he slurred.

"Let's dance. Forever. Just you and me," she whispered.

"Forever is a long time on Petra," he said, averting his eyes. Paris was flummoxed. He looked around at all the stunned faces, took a few breaths. He backed away and raised his hands toward the objecting mumble of the crowd.

"I have an announcement for you all!" he yelled in Greek.

Suddenly, every sound in the festive square was silenced.

"After many years of keeping you waiting, I have decided to be officially ordained," continued Paris.

His words were greeted with cheers, applause and whistles. Zoe stood to his side, feeling disregarded. She had taken a leap of faith and lost. Her eyes searched the blur of the gathered for some encouragement. She spotted Father Michael looking sad by his son's announcement. But Paris wasn't done yet.

"And there may be another surprise for you all tomorrow," he added, giving a very obvious glare toward Eleni. Unsettled, she cracked a tiny smile.

Zoe decided that was her cue to exit. She walked out of the square with her head down, but was unable to avoid Sophia's triumphant smile. Father Michael, Rita, Manos, Claudia and Aaron all turned to look at each other.

The folk band picked up their instruments and resumed playing their music. Paris continued staring at Eleni, who appeared embarrassed and out of place. Matter of fact, it felt as though the entire island was staring at her, too. The pressure was on. She looked mortified, struggling to keep it together. She politely broke their gaze, turning away from Paris and the crowd. Eleni continued her conversation with her mother and Grandpa Nikos, completely ignoring Sophia. In return, Sophia gave Paris and Father Michael an unyielding look. Feeling the forceful pressure of the hawk woman, they began choking on their clerical collars. They pulled to loosen them, catching their breaths.

EIGHTEEN

BLUE ZONE

Zoe felt a little better once she walked through her front door. The day was hot, and the cool interior of the villa felt as soothing as Yiayia's embrace. True, her grandma was absent for most of her life, but on the rare occasions when she was around, her presence more than made up for her delinquency. Zoe had memories of crying in her Yiayia's arms, distraught because of a dead beloved pet, or a scolding from her mom. Maria would shower an adolescent Zoe with kisses, whisper silly words of comfort to her, and always end with a final pep talk. "Chin up Zoe. Stand tall. Show your fists!"

"Show me how, Yiayia," Zoe said aloud, as she picked the splinters off the villa's broken doorframe.

Zoe could fix this. Her father was a master of tools and repairs. He had his own *Gepetto's Workshop* as he called it in their backyard, always working on something—when he wasn't rescuing the lives of animals—be it a birdhouse, or a rocking chair. Zoe loved watching him work on Sundays, waiting for an opportunity to be asked to lend a hand. Tomorrow, she would go to Manos' store to buy another lock, some wood filler, sandpaper and varnish. She had singlehandedly fixed the broken lock of her New York apartment, so this would be a walk in the park.

Zoe ambled into the stateroom and sat heavily on the sofa. She looked at her wristwatch.

"A sign, Yiayia… Please. Anything."

She removed the Cartier watch and turned to read the inscription. "Pethi mou" (*My child*). Its recent cleaning made it stand out more prominently than ever before. She examined further and noticed there was a third word. Surprised, she raised it closer to her eyes. "Pethi mou. *Paris*," it said.

"Oh Yiayia…" she sighed, then sobbed.

It was the city Maria's daughter (and Paris' mother) was born in. Zoe realized that Paris must have seen the dedication when he was cleaning the watch, but kept it to himself. It was the one word that connected Zoe and him. For years, she wore the Cartier going about her ordinary, everyday routine without being aware of this strong connection. The memories must have been a punishing reminder to her grandmother until the day Grandma Maria decided to unburden her sins by wrapping the watch around her granddaughter's wrist. She had even mentioned the watch in one of her letters. It seemed to have been an anniversary gift from Stefanos during their years spent in France. With that, Zoe once again saw an image of a young boy crying over his dead mother… a boy without his Yiayia.

She got up and went to the storeroom to take stock of the tools she needed for the repairs. Anything to keep herself busy or she might burst into flames. The first thing she discovered was a rolled-up blue and narrow Persian rug. It must have covered some hallway once upon a time, she thought. It felt soft to the touch, and it gave her an idea. She ran out carrying it, unrolled it on the lawn with a great big smile on her face. And then she saw them; spotted dried red stains all over the carpet. Curious, she raised her shoulders and humphed. All the same, she hurried upstairs to change into her sportswear and darted back out. Zoe felt like a tightly wound spring all day, her mind trapped, unable to sleep, unable to think straight. She needed so badly to relax, and it was about time she got back to her yoga workouts.

She sat on the Persian rug, took in a deep inhalation, placed her right hand on her belly and her left hand on her rib cage. She closed her eyes and exhaled slowly, making a "Haaa" sound, her breath soothing her like a breaking ocean wave.

"Relax Zoe," she said out loud.

Zoe continued her breathing exercise, feeling every wisp of air in through her nostrils and out through her lips. As she moved her right hand up to her chest, she was startled by a shuffling sound in the garden. She opened up her eyes and noticed Rita standing there with a worried look on her face. Zoe scanned the rest of the yard, searching for others, possibly Sophia. But thankfully, there was no one else with Rita.

"Hello darling," the old woman said timidly. "What you doin'?"

"Just relaxing. Saint Peter's Day doesn't agree with me," Zoe quipped.

"I see you leave Feast so sad, so I come see you al'right. No let Sophia or anybo'ty bully you, 'k? If Maria was here, she make't hell storm for you."

"Yeah, well, Yiayia ain't here. So..."

Rita attentively studied the blue and narrow carpet that

Zoe was exercising on. And like Zoe, she too raised her shoulders and humphed at the sight of it.

"You know, is strange for me talk to you like this. Let me sit…" added Rita. Before Zoe could react, the petite woman took the other half of the rug and squatted with remarkable agility.

"I need relax, too," Rita said, seriously. "They say announcement for Paris and Eleni wedding tomorrow. Will be double ceremony: first marriage, then ordination. That Sophia, she rushin' things like *craaazy*. And poor Eleni. I tell you she no want get married. Is all Sophia plan. So you no just relax and do nothing…"

"I'm trying to relax, Rita! And I don't want to yell at you," Zoe vowed. "Even though I have every right to do so——"

"At me? Why?"

Rita looked almost comical with her wide-eyed expression.

"The lies. The secrets. The agendas. You knew Paris was related to me and you said nothing."

Zoe laid on her back and brought her knees to her chest. She clasped her hands around them and closed her eyes. She continued her breathing exercises, hoping this relaxation was going to work. She heard boisterous shifting about and assumed that Rita was leaving. She looked, and to her surprise, saw the old woman mimicking the same position.

"So? You and Paris have some of Maria's blood. This is good thing——" she explained.

"A good thing!"

Rita turned her head to Zoe.

"Love is crazy. All best love is crazy. When I see way you look't Paris, I see crazy love in you eyes. I feel… hope——"

"Hope? How do you figure?"

The petite woman slowly sat upright, making Zoe follow suit.

"Maria and Stefanos had crazy love. Curse't love. Love against all odds... Remember when I tells you how time stand still when you meet love of your life...?"

Zoe nodded.

"When Maria love't Stefanos, the heavens shook and there was very *big* earthquake. Hundreds die. Houses destroy. And church bell clock stop. We think we punish'd from heavens... Sophia accuse't Maria and Stefanos for bringin' curse to Petra. And then people stop dyin'. No one age't... Time. Just. Stood. Still."

"Wait! What? That's!—" Zoe uttered in disbelief, unable to stop Rita.

"No more lies. No more secrets. I never want tell you lie. But Sophia force't us hide things from you," Rita went on. "Look me. I'm ninety-six years old and I no look it."

"What are you saying? This is insane... Because of their forbidden love affair, the island was... *cursed*?! That people stopped dying? And that Petra is... an island of... *immortals*? Is this what you... what all of you believe?"

"Believe me, dear Zoe. I know it sound *craaazy*. But when Maria and Stefanos leave for Europe, curse no break. Then Stefanos come back with daughter to save her because she sick, have fatal disease... He came back to give her... *life*. Only way people die on Petra is from accident, or..." Rita paused, unpleasant memories danced in her head.

"Suicide?" Zoe answered, struggling with this revelation. "Paris' mother... That wasn't an accident, was it?"

"I'm so sorry... Now you believe me?"

Zoe stood up, shuffled over to a lawn chair, and

collapsed. She needed to think, to process all this information. Her head hurt.

"This is too much. I believe that you believe it. I mean, I can understand a Blue Zone. But this...? All of this... it doesn't feel *natural*." She exhaled a long, anxious breath as she shook her head.

Rita got up and stood awkwardly, adjusting the corners of her shirt with her fingers while looking at the villa's door.

"I must get back to Feast. I left Dimitri alone... He waitin' for me—"

"Is Claudia still there?"

"No. Claudia no stay long. She leave."

Without any further comment, Rita left, or rather fled the villa.

Zoe ran upstairs to change before taking the high road into the heart of the island.

The weather cooled, the clouds marking the evening sky by the time Zoe arrived at the dig. Awake for over twenty-four hours now, the scenery seemed to be dancing around her. She teetered carefully over the shrubbery, feeling supremely fatigued by Rita's stories, which were doing summersaults in her head. She began doubting if the petite woman's visit even occurred. All of it felt so much like a dream.

She paused at the edge of the worksite and searched for Claudia. There was no sign of her in the trenches. Zoe approached the rusted out trailer, its door partly open. An air conditioning unit propped on the outer shell was humming noisily, working overtime. She noticed an electric cable line that connected a utility pole with the trailer. It was the first time Zoe was seeing the vehicle up close and it looked worse than it did from afar. It was a mess. The trailer barely held onto dear life, the rubber tires flattened to shreds, the hull greatly corroded by the sea salt air. But the interior was something else!

From what Zoe could tell, it looked to be Claudia's lab. Or, as she put it: a mad scientist's wet dream. The interior light was austerely dim, forcing Zoe's eyes squinting to adjust. Stacked against the windows were interconnected glass laboratory containers, beakers and Bunsen burners, specimen jars with tainted liquids and other indiscernible objects that floated inside. Claudia was bent over a microscope but didn't look surprised when she sensed Zoe approaching.

"You decide on my offer?" she asked.

"What's all this stuff?" Zoe countered.

"Sit down," Claudia replied, all business.

Cramped in one corner of the trailer was a couch covered with moving boxes, books and dossiers. Zoe found herself gawking at a taxidermy sheep on top of a pile of papers that returned a glassy-eyed stare at her. It was a bit too much for her to dare ask questions. She opted for a stool instead, dragging it next to Claudia.

"Drink?" offered Claudia, emptying a bottle of raki in her coffee mug.

"No, thank you," said Zoe. "So what's up with this place...?"

Claudia knocked back her drink, then let out a labored breath. She gestured at some jars.

"Long time ago, there was this old scientist who discovered that the fig trees native only to Petra were more than just *ordinary*, that their fruit secreted a special acid that reputedly restored youth. So he developed a potion, which he tested on farm animals. But all it did was put the islands' sheep into a very deep sleep for days... And, that there, was his favorite guinea pig. He named her Lolita. He was a poor, lonely old man..." Claudia recounted, grinning a little.

Zoe nodded, slowly putting two and two together.

"I just heard some nutty story from Rita. Apparently, this *here* is the island of the undead."

She waited for Claudia to reply. The German woman took her time, immersed in meticulous thought.

"As a scientist, I'm still baffled that time stands still since that earthquake ages ago. Rita told you the truth. Petra is a "time-free" zone—"

"That's impossible."

"Hard to believe, but it's all true—"

"How about the animals, the birds, the insects? Do they live forever?—"

"No. Just humans. That's what makes my work even more fascinating."

Zoe fidgeted while trying to think of her next question, something that could allow her to believe all his gobbledygook.

"And what about this Blue Zone you spoke about? Was it all lies?"

"Petra has all the workings of a true Blue Zone. Even before the earthquake, islanders were living very long, healthy lives, but—"

"How old are you?"

Claudia paused. For a moment, her blinking eyes were lost somewhere beyond the confines of the undersized trailer.

"I'm seventy-three," she answered, her voice crackling as proof to her answer.

Zoe gasped in disbelief. She was never much of a realist, though she was trying hard to get a grip on any shred of sanity.

"But you look my age! I can't for the life of me... I mean, *your face*... it just aged in front of me when we went out sailing. Is this what happened? When we crossed those buoys?"

"I can't even imagine what I look like with wrinkles," Claudia mumbled, trying to make light of the situation. Zoe struggled to come up with more questions.

"How about day? Night? All I see is the sun coming up and the sun going down every day..."

"The earth does turn, even on Petra. It is part of the world after all, and it must play by some of its rules. But Petra is unlike any other place on earth. Humans just don't die here. Remember when you asked me what I would do if I find this *elixir*? Well, Petra *is* the elixir. This entire island *is* eternal life."

Her last words were accentuated by a distant rumble of thunder.

"You're all fucken nuts!" exclaimed Zoe, feeling exhausted. She got up off the stool, pushed away the dossiers and files on the couch, and sat there, trying to rest from all this mind-boggling news. "Why isn't the island jammed with people, then?"

"The government has strict rules about settlers. Some *boat people* who make it across are allowed to stay temporarily to maintain the upkeep of some old homes, which they can't purchase, of course."

"*Boat people*... like ex-Prime Ministers, Hollywood actors, and American singers?"

"You're observant. We don't keep people from living, nor leaving. We just can't be overrun."

"So the only way you die is if you leave Petra or take your own life?"

"How do you think Stefanos passed away? He simply

got into a boat, rowed himself out of the bay away from the island's limits and—"

"Died after seeing my grandmother for the very last time!"

Claudia nodded.

"Poor Paris. He lost his grandfather."

"And I lost my uncle. Stefanos was my uncle—uncle Stephan. My father's brother. My dad kept a correspondence with him after the war... And one day I visited him here and after learning about this great discovery, well, it changed my future. The grants I received from Geo Campus in Berlin—and even from the Hellenic Armed Forces, plus the ERC—gave me the opportunity to live and conduct research here to finally find that alternative energy source that uncle Stephan was sent here for during the war. So that none of his life would be in vain." Claudia's words were concluded with the tapping of rain on the trailer's roof.

"My God... You're Paris' aunt?"

Zoe suddenly felt the whole of Petra leaning on her shoulders. She was exhausted.

"But you still haven't told me why and how you wanna purchase my villa? 'Specially since you don't have the right to do so..."

Zoe was spent and while she stared into nothing, her eyelids shut without realizing it. The cracks of thunder could not wake Zoe up, while the dance of the raindrops lulled her into much needed sleep. Claudia reached for a blanket and gently covered up the New Yorker castaway.

NINETEEN
EKATERINI

1988

"You should put the smaller clocks on the bottom and the bigger ones up top. Make it top-heavy. It'll make for a more striking perspective."

Catherine observed her boy looking at her with doubt, frowning, tight-lipped. Paris was nearing that age now, becoming her *little man*—the adolescent stage when a mother's hug was becoming too much of a nuisance. She desperately fought against it, but as her husband always said, "You can't keep him tangled in your skirts forever."

The boy now stood with his mother in the workshop, hovering over a crate filled with various kinds of broken clocks.

"It's a dumb idea," he replied.

"I think it will look very impressive."

"Father will never approve of it."

"Why not? The faithful often encase their hopes into offerings like those decorating Saint Peter's icon. How are these clocks any different? And you can display them in the narthex, not in the main temple. This way, Father will have no reason to deny you..."

"But they aren't enough clocks for that wall," he insisted, scooping a handful of clocks out of the container.

"Be patient. More will come your way. For as long as the spell lasts, people will keep sending them to you."

"Not if I fix the bell clock first," he challenged in a youthful determination that made his mother smile.

Catherine grabbed Paris and hugged him tightly, stroking his hair with abandon. How wonderful he smelled! The boy feigned annoyance and struggled to extricate himself from her embrace.

"Mama, that hurts."

She wiped away her tears before he could notice.

"Sorry. I love you, so I can't help myself."

Through the half closed door of the workshop, Catherine noticed Rita running toward the church. The sun was blasting hot and the little woman insisted on wearing her regular black "in mourning" outfit, along with her matching black headscarf.

"Ekaterini!" she yelled, looking for her.

Catherine exited the workshop and met Rita in the church's courtyard.

"Sotiri is leaving the island!" babbled the petite woman in Greek. "And he's taking his entire family with him! He's down at the pier with Tasia and the children."

Catherine didn't wait to hear more. She sprang down the road that led to the port, hoping to change Sotiri's mind. With him and his children gone, the school would be left only with six pupils, including Paris. Sotiri's family was not the first to leave the island in search of a different life, and she knew it was just a matter of time before the rest followed.

As she made her way down to the harbor, endless dirty

looks were thrown at Catherine, which bounced right off her. Having grown accustomed to such glares, the painful hatred that some islanders gave off had eventually become a constant part of her daily life. Catherine was the German's daughter, as well as their children's teacher. Her arranged marriage to their priest was the saving grace Stefanos had aimed for.

"For your own good. He's a good man," her father had endlessly repeated.

Thankfully, not all islanders were tangled in Sophia's web of repugnance. Sophia's rage was relentless, even though she feared Catherine, as much as she hated her. "Ekaterini" (*Catherine*) was Maria's daughter and she could *see* the future like her mother. Interestingly enough, most of the animosity expressed toward her came from the *oldest* of the old people—the ones who had benefited the most from the curse. She understood they were afraid that she could deprive them of immortality at any moment by simply breaking the spell. Catherine was, after all, the "witch" and the "Nazi's daughter". Though she knew she was actually powerless, she was just as cursed as everyone else. But she did not try to dissuade them of the contrary. It was the only leverage Catherine had, her arsenal for keeping Sophia and the rest of them at bay.

Now the daughters and sons, and granddaughters and grandsons of Petra were a different story. The children had escaped the tragedy of war and the grandchildren were innocent, devoid of any superstition. Her students absolutely loved her and they were her anchors for enduring her unasked-for life. And they were slipping through her fingers like running water, one drop at a time.

~

She spotted the family huddled at the dock next to a pile of chests and suitcases, Sotiri negotiating the travel arrangements with a navy official by the supply boat.

Tasia noticed Catherine approaching and smiled with trembling lips, while her two girls ran to greet their teacher. Tasia was not a local; she was from the island of Rhodes. And ever since her arrival on Petra, she had struck a deep friendship with Catherine. The two women hugged long and hard, Tasia and her daughters breaking into tears.

Sotiri turned to look at them, a brooding man, not as talkative or outgoing as the rest. Tasia had expressed to Catherine her fears of this very departure for quite some time now, foreseeing this day from the relentless ruminating that was going on in her husband's head. And Sotiri had been sulking a whole lot lately. And here they were now. This, was actually happening.

"Where will you go? What will you do?" Catherine asked Sotiri.

He turned away, feeling like a heel. No one else on this island had Catherine's chains that bound her for eternity on this piece of rock. And she wanted to leave, to soar free, more than anyone else on Petra. And Sotiri knew this well.

"Anywhere is better than here," he said. "I want a future for my children. This place has no future. It is stuck in the past. It avoids death, but offers no life. And we want to live. Not forever... But to be... *free*."

It would be a lie to dispute him, she reasoned in silence. And it would also be selfish.

~

She stood at the pier and watched as the boat taking away her friends was now just a shadow against the island. She wanted to renounce Petra too, and maybe today was the right day to do so.

"You will die if you leave the island," she was constantly told. She was thirteen when she confronted her father, screaming, on why she could not join her classmates to yet another school excursion to Andoriani. It was the same day she was informed about this "cursed fairy tale", that she was stuck on Petra for life.

Catherine returned home with heavy steps, avoiding eye contact with everyone who dared look at her. What she feared most was seeing any form of happiness in others. The pain was worse now, freedom felt sweeter than ever, and she needed to do one last thing. She continued past the village, following the ridge toward the northern shore. The green slope of shrubbery below her, the blue Aegean beyond and the majestic sky above, all painted the imaginary bars of her cage that mercilessly imprisoned her. She paused to look and all she could see was the face of her mother, frozen in time, smiling at her from the picture frames on her father's walls. Catherine would never see Rome, nor Paris, nor any place else. She felt the sting, but refused to set her tears free. The time of tears was over, she vowed. And with a few strides, she had arrived. Stefanos was sitting on the porch, observing her approach. The strong northern wind ruffled her dress wildly, her hair swaying like Medusa's around her pale face.

Catherine felt both sorrow and anger, fixing her fists straight down her hips. And, of course, she knew he was *seeing* Maria. "I'm nothing like her!" she had said on countless occasions, every time her father would point to their similarities. And yet today, she would prove him right. *I have never been more like her until today*, she thought.

"It's been a while, stranger," he said to her, smiling. "I would have cooked something if I knew you were coming."

"I'm not staying long," she retorted. "I just came from the port. Today I bid farewell to Tasia and her family. Sotiri took them away. You understand why they left, don't you? Why all of them leave... And I know you admire them for it. They do the one thing you cannot."

"You know why—"

"Spare me the story. Today I finally understood why my mother abandoned me."

Stefanos shut his mouth, said nothing, listened to her, looking bent under the weights of the past.

"I don't know if everything you told me about her is true. If indeed you have no news of her... But I wish you to tell her one day, that I understand, but I do not forgive. You tell her that," she concluded, and turned to leave.

"Catherine... *Ekaterini!*" he called after her. "Stay a while. You're upset..."

"I cannot stay. I must be elsewhere," she replied without looking at him, keeping her stride steady.

She thought him to be too German to read her sentiment, to guess her intentions. And in the long run, she would prove to him that she was as cruel as her mother.

On her way back to the church, she walked past Paris who was out kicking a football with five other kids. The boy was too engrossed in his game and did not spot his mom. The kids were shouting insults, pushing, elbowing each other, falling, raising hell—kids being kids. She knew these kids were Paris' last remaining peers on the island. She slowed down and hid under the protection of a fig tree, but did not call on him. He looked so very happy. Yet, she was in turmoil. She didn't want Paris to see her like this. She watched him, absorbing his every move. Catherine resisted her tears once more, and eventually pried herself away as she continued undetected toward Saint Peter's Church.

She knew by the shadows cast on the hot cobblestones that her husband, Michael would still be at the port café playing backgammon with Dimitri. She also knew that she now had the full attention of God and the spirits of Petra. With the clock tower workshop door bent open, she invited herself to the winding scaffoldings all the way to the top. As she reached the gallery next to the bell clock, she rested for a moment. Paris' tool kit sat there opened, testament to her little magician's struggle to find the right magic potion. She grinned big.

"Follow your heart, my boy," Catherine murmured, finally wiping a runaway tear. She knew Paris would be free one day and that he would leave the island, untouched by the curse. If she remained on Petra, she would become a terrible mother, eventually passing her shackles and chains to him. More tears flowed. She raised her head and looked at the big bell above the clock. She remembered sitting on Rita's knees listening to the unbelievable tales of her parents and of the curse, countless of times. How she so loved hearing their love story as a little girl; of her parents' magical kiss and of the ensuing earthquake. And she was convinced that only love could break the spell. She had foreseen it. She herself was not given the opportunity for true love. Catherine felt the utmost tenderness for her husband Michael, but she had never truly fallen in love with him. And no one, except for God and the internal consciousness of Petra knew this.

"No more, no more," she whispered, as her voice broke. Catherine was now the little girl with waterfall eyes. She stepped onto the edge of a plank and looked down at the church square. Instinctively, she did the sign of the cross.

"Forgive me," she uttered.

She felt no fear. She had no doubt. For her, this was the magic potion that would stop the pain. She took one more step and flew free into the heavens.

TWENTY
FORBIDDEN FRUIT

Zoe oddly dreamt of New York, that she was back there, managing her store, handling the daily flow of customers, chit-chatting and exchanging neighborhood gossip. Surprisingly, two of her buyers were actually Manos and Aaron. And even Rita showed up, shopping for sexy pants!

Zoe would end her day rolling down the shutters of her establishment, but not before walking to the pier in Astoria to take the ferry to the island of Petra. Paris would be finishing his evening service at Saint Peter Church and they would later meet at the villa. They would have dinner with their two children, eating and conversing about their day. Zoe imagined this from her own perspective, although she was her daughter at the same time, just as her brother was a little Paris. She felt happy, though, an alarming darkness loomed outside the windows. All of a sudden, violent thunder crashed in her dream, springing her back to reality.

It took Zoe a while to realize that she was now awake. Her head weighed a hundred pounds and her eyes were twirling like a majorette baton. Raindrops danced hard on the trailer's roof, the overcast sky enabling a pale light through the windows. She smelled coffee. Claudia was stirring the brew in a pot, propped over one of her laboratory burners.

"*Guten morgen,*" she greeted.

"What do you mean, *morning*?" Zoe asked, rubbing her eyes.

"Never have I seen anyone sleep like that. And it rained fiercely all night. Not to mention the thunder rolls... But nothing could disturb you."

"I slept here all night?"

"Weren't for the clouds, the sun would be up and shining above the horizon just about now. *Some* summer storm... As rare as they come."

Zoe shifted on the couch, causing files and documents to spill on the floor.

"Sorry."

"My problem for never getting rid of anything." Claudia leaned down to pick up the mess. "Always afraid I might lose something important."

"Where'd you sleep?"

She pointed to a curtain on her end of the trailer.

"I have a bed in there."

"Do you have a toilet?"

Claudia motioned to the door next to her workbench. Zoe squeezed into the bathroom that was no bigger than an airline lavatory.

Zoe hadn't realized how hungry she was until she wolfed down a box of not-so-fresh crackers. She followed that up with a long and thankful sip of coffee. Zoe still felt her brain a wee bit foggy, but the hot brew warmed her insides just right. She palmed her hands tightly around the coffee mug, which made her feel oddly protected, even for the tiniest of moments. As illusions went, this one was welcomed.

"Feeling better?" Claudia inquired.

"I think so. What time is it?"

"Hard to tell in this weather."

All of a sudden, they heard the distant chime of the church bell. As unplanned prompts go, this, for Zoe, was a doozy.

"It's quite late in the morning, actually," Claudia corrected herself.

Zoe sprang to her feet, almost spilling her coffee.

"The service!" she shouted. "He's getting ordained! And married!"

As she darted for the door, Claudia rushed to her side.

"*Keine gut Idee* in this downpour," she argued.

Zoe said nothing. She pushed the door and jumped out, splashing onto thick mud. She ran as fast as she could, jumping and landing on clearings, avoiding the rain-filled trenches. She crossed her way over to the main dirt road and made tracks to the village.

"Not a good idea in any weather!" Claudia shouted after her, entirely aware of Zoe's foolhardy intentions.

The muddy road was tailor-made for a nightmare, where the dreamer remains stuck, running in the same spot no matter their effort. But Zoe kept pushing through the relentless deluge. The dirt road had now become a river of heavy mud rushing down along with her. She felt the piercing rain hitting her head like bullets, her clothes sticking onto her skin like wet paper. Zoe ignored the punishing elements. "You're one with Mother Nature," she repeated to herself as she sloshed through ankle-deep sludge water.

She had no idea why she jumped out of the trailer like that; a question tolling strong in her head, the closer she got. She was convinced that Paris was about to make some serious mistakes, thus committing himself to an unhappy life for all eternity. He did not wish to become a priest. She knew that, he knew that, the whole island knew that. Though he did have a saintly singing voice, she reflected. And he surely did not love Eleni. In spite of everything, it was an arranged marriage and, as everyone knows, they never work. Or at least that's how she bargained in her head.

Zoe had to put a stop to all this madness once and for all. Now the "why" had a simple explanation. But the "how" hadn't been thought out just yet. One option was to simply rush into the ceremony and kibosh it. At least that was her reckless, unthought-out plan. Would she enter the church and shout out his name like in the finale of *The Graduate* as Benjamin raced to win Elaine's heart? Although initially ecstatic with their triumphant success, both Dustin Hoffman and Katharine Ross' characters became increasingly uncomfortable as they journeyed toward their uncertain future. But that's the normal ups and downs of love and life, Zoe reckoned.

Her employee Katie's voice was back again, coming along for the ride. She whispered to Zoe all the things that were too embarrassing for her to face. "You don't want to lose those blue eyes to the church, do you?" Katie argued. "You should have done the nasty with him when you had the chance," she continued. "He's my cousin," Zoe shot back. "Albert Einstein married his first cousin," Katie argued, Zoe wondering how she even knew that?! She's a naïve, wet behind the ears Millennial, after all.

Her shoes were wrecked by the time she reached the cobblestones. The heavy rain kept falling, but she paid no attention to it. Zoe was truly soaked past any feeling. A blurry curtain made the view of Petra ripple open like swinging drapes in a theater. The roads were devoid of people, but as she paced into the church square, she came across an unknown elderly man who held tightly onto his purple umbrella. He let out a wail and collapsed against some tables, but Zoe didn't stop to help him. "Sorry, but I'm on a mission," she thought, then covered the remaining steps toward the church completely barefoot.

She paused under the shelter of the narthex to catch her breath, letting the rain drip off her and onto the marble tiles.

She could hear the chanting from within the temple and for a moment, she froze. Was she insane? Was she wrong? Was she the villain of this story? Through the stained glass doors, she could see the silhouette of the congregation, spotted by the flames of burning candles. Zoe was a hot mess. Her dignity was treading on the bottom of her barrel, so how much worse could it get? She reminded herself that in Greek Orthodox weddings the priest does not ask if the guests have any objections to the marriage, prompting her to push through the royal doors and put an end to these proceedings, pronto.

She entered, and there was no turning back. And of course, she knew fully well that she would be the star of the spectacle—a fitting conclusion to her equally spectacular arrival to the island just days ago. The whole of Petra was huddled in there, jammed to the rafters. It was sweltering, almost impossible to breathe. It felt more like a Native American sweat lodge than an actual Greek Orthodox ceremony. Worshippers were busily flapping hundreds of hand fans to cool off without success. Sweat was pouring down every soul's face. And once more, they all gawked at Zoe.

Father Michael stood at the altar, The Good Book open in his hands. He looked at Zoe, openmouthed. Paris was positioned near him. The front part of the nave was crammed, Zoe barely making out Eleni through the crowd. She was dressed all in white. Next to the young girl was her mother, and of course, her grandparents. Needless to say, Sophia eyeballed Zoe. Finally, she spotted her two favorite allies—Rita and Dimitri in his wheelchair—both smiling happily, bringing up the head of the nave. A deafening silence reigned. So much so that Zoe could clearly hear the drips and drops of rain flowing from her soaked body and onto the red ceremonial carpet under her feet. Father Michael broke the silence by resuming his reciting.

"Oh God most pure, Author of all creation, Who through Your man-befriending love transformed a rib of Adam the forefather into a woman, and blessed them and said, 'Increase and multiply, and have dominion over the earth,' and, by the conjoining, declared them both to be one member, for because of this a man shall forsake his father and his mother, and shall cleave unto his wife, and the two shall be one flesh—and whom God has joined together let not man put asunder."

She locked eyes with Paris. *Here I am,* she thought, hoping he would read her mind. For an instant, she believed that he felt her message, too. But then he looked away, toward Eleni, shattering Zoe's resolve. As Zoe backed away and turned to leave, she heard Father Michael faltering on his chant, followed by a condemning murmur rising in the church. Zoe pushed through the swinging doors and exited to the narthex. She fumbled with the knobs of the outer doors, her eyes burning but unable to feel any tears. She was drenched to her very soul. A shout slammed her back like a fist.

"Leave now! Get off this island!"

She sensed her cheeks burning. Fully ignited, Zoe turned to face Sophia. She had never seen her in a dress before that was not the traditional 'in mourning' black, this one having some cutesy flower-like patterns.

"Go back to the wedding!" Zoe hissed through her teeth, not wanting to jinx the joining of her granddaughter with the prized groom of Petra.

"It's a sin!" shouted Sophia. "It's a sin what you're doing. You shall never be with Paris. You shall both burn in hell."

"I know it was you who stole my Yiayia Maria's letters from Stefanos' house, delivering them to me. Was that your way of saving our souls?"

"Go back to America! You don't belong here!"

She took a few forceful steps toward Sophia. Zoe had no idea how she looked, but the hawk woman retreated two steps away.

"Who do you think you are?" Zoe challenged. "Don't tell me what to do. I belong here. This is my Yiayia's home… *my* home."

"Maria brought upon a curse to Petra. You're unclean like her."

"No Sophia. You and your hatred cursed this place," Zoe sneered boldly. "But I'll end your curse. I know it. I have seen it in my dreams."

She saw terror in Sophia's eyes for the very first time. Truly surprising, Zoe thought. Not wanting to ruin a perfect closing argument, she turned her back on the hawk woman and exited the church.

Aaron appeared out of nowhere, waiting for Zoe just outside, purple umbrella in hand.

"It's raining, ma'am. Allow me to escort you home," he greeted, offering his elbow under the opened umbrella. Zoe took Aaron's arm and they mucked through the rain.

~

Aaron collapsed his purple umbrella just under the broken doorframe as Zoe stumbled into the villa.

"Come in," she encouraged. "I have no idea what I could offer you. As you know, I've been living here with one foot in New York. Never quite made this place home, so I didn't think of stocking the kitchen, haaa!"

"I'm sure we'll manage something," Aaron affirmed, grinning at her. He entered the house.

"The kitchen's over there," she pointed. "Knock yourself out."

She turned to give Aaron an intense look that suddenly had him feeling really awkward. Before he could utter a word, she approached Aaron and wrapped her hands around him. She pressed her lips on his, in a long, deep kiss. Aaron kissed Zoe back. Moments later, she stepped back, studying him with a charming smile.

"Just in case you're the *real thing*. I didn't want to miss my chance," Zoe said. "I'll go and change into something dry."

As she climbed up the stairs, Aaron watched her wholly hypnotized, the taste of sweet rain on his lips.

~

The kitchen was better stocked than Zoe realized, mostly from the easy efforts of a few good friends like Rita and

Dimitri. Aaron found enough supplies to fix them a few ham sandwiches, complimented by a fresh infusion of tsai tou vounou (*mountain tea*). As summer storms go, this was a nippy one, and unusually so. A kettle of hot tea was a welcomed idea. He added lemon slices into the cups for a touch of finesse. Now in her yoga wear with a towel wrapped around her head, Zoe hunkered down on the sofa. Aaron served the food and tea on the coffee table. He dragged an armchair next to the sofa and sat facing her. They enjoyed the sandwiches in silence and sipped their tea, listening to the downpour outside. Aaron took a slice of lemon and begun sucking on it.

"So you're selling this place?" he asked.

"Yes. I think it's best I take the first offer and go."

"Back in the church, I saw you talking to that Sophia woman—"

"You know her?"

"I've been living on Petra for many years. I've made some friends with the locals... Manos being a good one—"

"Manos is the best!"

"But that Sophia woman... I didn't know she even existed until just before you arrived on the island. She took us all by storm—all the guests of Petra, I mean—spilling tales of dread about you. About wishing to drive you away from here. She said you're dangerous, cursed and that you would break the spell that keeps us all alive..."

"Do you believe her?"

"None of us who found shelter here really knows how this all *works*. But none of us believes in magic or curses. That's all superstition. And let me tell you this: that Sophia woman is *not* the island."

"She seems to think so."

"She is not Petra." Aaron shook his head.

"I don't care about her..." Zoe's eyes glazed.

"Paris...?" he asked.

She nodded.

"Paris is *my*—"

"I know. And you fell for him."

Aaron watched Zoe as she fell quiet, noticing her lower lip tremble.

"There are too many examples in history where love prevails all. Didn't go so well for my old pal Jerry Lee. But there was also an age issue there…"

Aaron stopped as if he heard something.

"Listen…" he said. They both stood still, ears focused on the silence. "The rain stopped. Summer is back!"

With the noise of the downpour now silenced, the final flow of the villa's storm drains was a welcoming sound. She was about to say something just when the jolly chimes of Saint Peter's resounded over the stillness, instantly crushing her mood and thoughts.

"Well, it's all over now," she commented, sipping her tea, keeping herself busy and distracted.

"I'm so sorry," he said.

They waited in silence for the chimes to end. When they finally did, Zoe opened her mouth to say something again, but this time she let out an undignified yawn.

"I'm more tired than I thought." She yawned again. "What kind of tea is this?"

"Some tea I found in your cupboard. Plus some herbs from my garden…"

"Aaron, you're so naughty—"

"Oh, no! It's medicinal. It will help you relax."

He got up and took her cup, just as she laid back, her head resting on the end pillow.

"Please think it all through before you make another rash decision," he murmured, in a comforting voice.

She smiled and said nothing as he approached the front door.

"And nothing is over until the fat lady sings," he added, smiling, finger gunning her with both hands. Aaron then left the building.

Zoe turned her attention to the old chandelier hanging from the ceiling, contemplating the size of her problems, compared to the enormity of the cosmos. She was emotionally exhausted. She pictured Paris kissing Eleni. Would they leave the island for their honeymoon, or would a honeymoon be completely inappropriate for an ordained priest? "Can you see me as a Priest's wife, Yiayia?" she said aloud and laughed. She had her heart broken before. Time heals everything, she thought. But only away from this place, where time ticks like it's supposed to.

Zoe got up and ran upstairs to her bedroom. It was time for all this to end. She changed to her jeans and runners, the evening light settling on the villa's windows. She marched out of the house with the title deed to the villa tucked once again in her back pocket.

TWENTY-ONE
BREAKING THE SPELL

The idea was to first go to Manos' mini market to call Katie and to let her know that she'd be coming home very soon. Then, she would find Claudia or Kostas and sell them the villa—or to anyone else who'd be interested for that matter. In her mind, any sale would do. Zoe simply needed the money to save her business and her life back home, and fast! She would then go to *Mr. Mayor* to get him to do his job.

As she walked the streets, she prepared herself for the scrutiny she would get by all who had witnessed her humiliation in church an hour earlier. Zoe now understood, at least partially, what it was really like for Maria, Stephan and Catherine to live here. To her surprise, the streets were empty. The sun had fallen and there wasn't a soul in sight, which suited her just fine. As Zoe crossed the plaza, she noticed the lights were still on in the church, the temple glowing against the evening darkness like a castle made up of amber. She looked up to the workshop and the scaffoldings and could see Paris moving about, up by the belfry. Zoe slowly scaled the planks toward the clock, her steps carefully measured, as the wood under her feet was soggy and slippery from the rainfall. She spotted Paris trying to retrofit an old three-foot cog, totally immersed to the task at hand. She couldn't avoid noticing how much more handsome he looked in his new priestly black outfit.

Paris didn't hear her coming. Zoe was just about to call his name when the plank creaked under her footing. He turned around and was surprised to see her. She felt as if it had been forever since she'd seen him last and tried so hard to control her choking feelings. For her, their personal separation began on the battlements of the castle just before he turned his heart to someone else. She grinned and produced a pen out of her pocket.

"I brought a pen this time," she said. "So no more excuses."

He placed the cog by his feet and wiped his hands with a cloth as she unfolded the deed. Without showing any emotion, Paris took the document and pen from her hands, skimmed through the fine print, then backed the paper against the tower's wall and signed it. And with that simple stroke of a pen, there was a new serenity in his face. He no longer looked at her disapprovingly.

"There you go," he said, handing her the signed title deed and pen.

She didn't expect to feel devastated, but she automatically did.

"Where's everybody?" she asked in a trembling voice.

"At the pier, bidding goodbyes to their loved ones. The navy ship is taking the guests back to Andoriani."

"And here you are, tinkering with your clock. I didn't expect that. Tell me something. All these years after your mother died, why did you stay? Knowing fully well that time could never be… *fixed*?"

"Hope, I guess. Without it, I really had nothing. For

years, my mom anxiously prayed I could fix the clock and break the spell. And when she couldn't take the guilt anymore of knowing she was the child of a cursed love affair, of a cursed island, she ended her life. It was no freak accident when she fell off the scaffolding—"

"You knew?"

"Yes. My mom jumped. After that, Stefanos secluded himself and spoke to no one."

Paris paused, then turned away. He hobbled a few steps toward the broken bell clock.

"Where's your wife?" Zoe asked, matter-of-factly.

"I didn't marry Eleni. We talked before the ceremony and we both agreed. She was being pressured to marry me... It never would have worked, anyway. Of course, hell hath no fury like a Sophia spurned. Now *that* storm will endure a while..."

Zoe began tingling all over. She heard Katie screaming inside her head.

"But I heard the bells?" she said.

"Oh yes. Rita and Dimitri got married instead! It was about time." Paris smiled big. "And as you can imagine, Sophia was not pleased with that either."

"What? No way! I don't believe it." Zoe was above the moon. "I'm so happy for them. They deserve it!"

"I took my vows as a priest, however. I've been ordained."

Two notches up, one notch down for Zoe, she thought.

"So it's official," he continued. "I'm a watch-making priest with nothing to repair, but with all the time in the world."

Zoe dared another step toward Paris and heard the wood protest under her weight.

"Be careful," he said. "The planks are damp from the rain and it's been a while since I replaced these—"

Before he could finish, the tower of scaffoldings let out an alarming sound followed by the metallic twisting of the iron supports. She freaked as the entire structure swayed under her feet. It was collapsing and they were going to die!

"Zoe!" he shouted, extending his hand to her. "Hold on!"

She leaped on him, securing herself in his embrace. Paris lead Zoe to a rope that was attached to the bell tower. They could hear planks and iron rods bouncing off the church square below as the scaffolding support moaned and detached from the tower. Paris pulled the rope with his free hand and lifted Zoe under the archway of the bell chamber. They landed safely next to the bell just as they heard the thunderous collapse below.

In the faint illumination of the church stained glass windows, they stared at each other so closely and so intimately, their intense breathing stroked each other's lips. But little did they know that lives were being shattered in the village beneath them, their hypnotic hold completely blocking out the horrific sounds of a strong earthquake.

"I think you saved my life," she said, out of breath.

"You saved mine," he replied.

The moment was beyond words. They embraced hard and sunk into each other, his hand grabbing the nape of her neck before raking his fingers through her hair. He pulled her head closer to his face and parted her lips with his mouth. She thrust him down and onto the surface of the gantry, straddling him, at no time abandoning the kiss. She found his free hand and guided it under her shirt. He let out a surprised grunt, but didn't let go.

This is happening! she screamed in her head. She made space between them as she struggled to pull his priestly garment up to his chest, wondering what she'd discover underneath. Panting heavily with short, quick breaths, they paused momentarily to look at each other. There was absolutely no regret in their eyes. He took her back into his arms again, locking his lips with hers once more. Mesmerized and spellbound, Zoe and Paris completely overlooked the unexpected swaying of the tower, the bell tolling, the whole of Saint Peter's Church shaking on its very foundations.

They held onto each other as the temple rattled and shuddered around them. The bell chimed a toll the likes of which they had never heard before. The church's mortar cracked as chandeliers, candle and votive stands swayed wildly, icons smashed and vitro stained glass windows shattered onto the marble floor.

"I love you!" she screamed in his ear.

"I love you, too," he replied, and they both smiled blissfully.

Nothing else mattered. They finally felt the houses of Petra shaking around them, too. They could hear rooftop tiles showering the streets with debris. And as the screams of the people at the pier reached the bell clock tower, the earth rumbled with no end in sight. Again, none of it mattered. Not knowing what the next day will bring—if there was even going to be a next day—Zoe turned to Paris and discovered a new world underneath his priestly outfit. An exploration that ran the duration of the earthquake and the two aftershocks that followed.

The dust of the island rose like a mist that glowed under the moonlight and lingered a long while over the rooftops. The lights in the church flickered but remained alight. They watched it all from the belfry, huddled and safe in the warmth of their bodies.

"Did we do all that?" Zoe asked. "I still can't believe it..."

"In all my life, I never once experienced an earthquake on Petra. And we have tremors in Greece all the time, in all corners of the country. I only heard stories about the *big one* that started it all..." Paris paused, his torso suddenly tensing under her arms. "Listen... What's that sound?—"

"What?"

He hushed her. Cogs were turning under their feet. The clock's big metallic dial moved the space of a whole minute with a loud clang.

TWENTY-TWO
HEAVEN HAS FALLEN

Saint Peter's Church bell chimed twelve times. The disheveled lovers came down the stairs cautiously, holding hands and inspecting the new cracks on the wall inside the bell clock tower. Once inside the church, Paris quickly put out a small fire that was ignited by fallen candles. A muffled vibration buzzed in Zoe's hip pocket as her smartphone returned from the dead. She pulled it out and found more than three hundred text messages waiting for her. She looked at her wristwatch and realized it was now ticking. Zoe then remembered the title deed to the villa. She checked her pockets, but it wasn't on her. She tried to think when she lost it, but drew a blank. Zoe and Paris then exited Saint Peter's and took the road to the pier.

The cobblestones were covered with rubble, fronts of houses were fissured, street lamps and electric poles dangled over. Just then, Zoe noticed the lights were on in Manos' mini market, a shadow stumbling about inside. She entered to find the place in ruins. The shelves had been dislodged from the walls, canned goods and broken bottles blanketed the floor. The store reeked of raki, ouzo and other liquors.

Doubled over in a corner against the wall was Aaron, clutching his belly and trembling with shock. Zoe rushed to his side and kneeled close, observing the transformation of his face with disbelief. His hair had grown white, his cheeks had sunk and the lines of time filled his face with deep wrinkles. She called out his name several times, trying desperately to get his attention without success. Zoe cupped his face in her hands, as Aaron struggled to recognize her. Then, the sparkle returned to his eyes.

"Zoe…? That shook us good, didn't it? I was minding the store for Manos. He went to the port to see his family off and BAM!"

"Oh Aaron, I'm so sorry…" she choked up, unsure of what she was even sorry for. Paris knelt next to her.

"Are you alright?" he asked Aaron.

Aaron began to cough violently into his fist. He wiped his lips with his sleeve and looked at his wrinkled hand. He frantically scanned the floor, then pointed to some broken glass.

"Hand me that, will you?" he demanded of Paris.

Part of a store shelf display, the mirrored glass had been shattered into pieces. Paris picked up a piece and shyly handed it to Aaron. He looked at his reflection as Zoe held her breath. Aaron dropped the mirror and offered up a bitter smile.

"Guess there was some magic behind all of this," he said, chuckling. "I'm afraid I wasn't respectful enough, took it for granted. We all did."

"I'm so sorry Aaron," Zoe muttered again.

"That's how life goes, ma'am. We have no say in it."

"We must go," Paris stressed to Zoe.

"Go ahead," said Aaron. "I'll be fine. Once I get my

wind back, I'll be back on my feet in two shakes. So go rattle and roll!"

Zoe leaned in and kissed him on his cheek before joining Paris, who was already on his way out.

∼

The port was a disaster zone. The storefronts had collapsed and the road was laced with rubble. Burst water pipes were now fountains dispensing drinking water to the sea. Strangely, the lights in most establishments still worked, offering adequate brightness to the unfolding drama, with additional lighting being provided by the navy frigate's spotlights.

The harbor's water seemed to be boiling, lashing the port with foaming waves. Most of the fishing boats had been dislodged from their moorings with many scattered away, belly-up in the sea. The islanders and visitors were drenched and had retreated to shelter provided by the port's shops, as others were shouting pleas for help. The navy personnel suddenly had their hands full. The scene was tragic. Locals were visibly showing their age, shaking and moaning, shrivelled up in the arms of their daughters and sons. Women and men over one hundred years old were now dying. Others were collapsing, too weak to stand on their own. Father Michael was on the deck of the frigate, bent over a dying man and administering last rites.

Zoe and Paris reached the port and stopped dead in their tracks. She spotted Manos sitting at the fishing bait shop, surrounded by his children and grandchildren. She yelled out his name and made her way to him through the pitiful crowd. His family was a collection of worried frowns, though Manos was smiling, busily trying to reassure them. He looked pleased to see Zoe. He took her hand before she could utter a word.

"Thank you," he said. "You're a blessing to this island. Don't listen to anyone who would say otherwise."

"Are you alright?!"

He winced and let out a cough.

"I'm getting a little scolding from my liver, poor fellow. But don't worry. Me and him go a long way back. We'll settle this... What's important is that I'm now finally free and in the hands of God. We all are..."

Zoe turned to look at Paris, only to see him surrounded by clutching hands. People were dragging him toward their sick and dying parents, desperately wanting his blessings and absolutions. Zoe stood up to join him when she felt a tag on her shoulder. She didn't recognize the woman standing behind her. Yet she was sure she had seen her days before, past the red buoys that surrounded the island.

"Claudia?" she questioned.

The German woman's hair was now white, her cheeks amply puffed and marked with freckles.

"Time caught up with me," she replied, smiling woefully.

"Stop it. You look fine. A real cougar, I say!" Zoe smiled encouragingly at her, too baffled by everything and unable to react. "How do you feel?"

"Upset. This earthquake wiped out the phenomenon before I could discover its roots."

"Uhmmm, me and Paris were, well, when it started, we were together, and he and I, well, uhmmm," Zoe mumbled awkwardly as Claudia tried desperately to follow along. "I think Paris and I broke the curse," Zoe concluded in a huff, waiting for judgment.

Claudia smirked. "I admit that living in Petra for so long immersed me in the local lore, I stand guilty of that.

But what kind of scientist would I be to believe that you fucking your blood relative would lift a decades-old curse of eternal time on this island? I say, what an earthquake brought to the place, another earthquake took away. It may well happen again, so that I will still have a job here."

Suddenly, Claudia's eyes focused beyond Zoe and were instantly covered in tears. Zoe turned to see the navy chief surgeon approaching them. He was oozing with a new attitude, Zoe noticed. Was it an actual... *emotion*? Claudia left Zoe's side and ran toward the man, joining him in a passionate embrace. He stroked her hair and lifted her by the chin to meet her tearful eyes.

"Sooo?" she asked.

"Time has been good to you, Miss Mueller. I don't have to feel like a dirty old man with you anymore. Finally, after all these years," snorted the navy chief surgeon.

They hugged and kissed long. It seemed like they had done this many times before. Like a whole lot. Zoe's jaw dropped with delight.

The visitors were blaming the earthquake for the demise of their loved ones. Zoe caught a glimpse of the ailing peering at her with their dark and scared eyes, pointing and mouthing curses. She looked for Paris, who was well beyond her reach. That's when she spotted Sophia coming straight for her, supported left and right by her husband, her daughter, and granddaughter, Eleni. The hawk woman could barely walk, her face heavily crumpled, yet her claws still glowed in her eyes, the crowds turning into a chorus that surrounded Sophia and Zoe at the center.

"Sinners!" yelled Sophia, shooting Zoe and Paris an evil look. "What have you done?" Sophia then addressed the audience. "I told you all, we should have not allowed her on the island. But you didn't believe me, and you wouldn't listen. Now look... This is all her doing!"

"Deport her now!" shouted an angry voice from the crowd.

Zoe didn't bother to see who it was. The crowd was a tapestry of faces, all of them one creature. "For it takes just one person who yells the loudest to lead a Greek mob," her grandmother Maria once told her while watching *Zorba the Greek* on television.

"Deport the priest, too!" added another anonymous yeller.

"Quiet!" Manos roared, as he stumbled out of the mob. "Anyone lays their hands on them must first go over my dead body. We will not repeat the sins from our past!"

Sophia gave him a filthy look, raising her voice above his, pleading to the crowd.

"We can overcome this! It can be fixed. Things can go back to normal, right? Right!"

Nikos took his wife by her waist and looked at her fondly.

"Darling, listen to me. We need to take back our lives—"

"And live our lives like mortals again," added Manos.

Father Michael entered the circle. He stood by Zoe and addressed the crowd in English.

"*'If anyone keeps My word he will never see death.'*" Alas Sophia, you are not God. None of us are. We've kept the secret of Petra far too long."

"Sophia, it's over!" a new voice exclaimed.

"Yes, let it go. We've had enough!" someone else shouted.

"We're tired. Some of us just want to die..." joined another.

A sudden shriek brought the quarrel to a halt. The crowd moved aside and made way for Rita to pass. The petite woman looked distraught. She was barefoot, a shawl hanging crookedly over her black nightgown, and her hair was in disarray. She, like the rest of the islanders, had the marks of her years now on her facial features and her feet were wounded from running barefoot over the debris.

"Dimitri is dead!" she bellowed.

Zoe approached and hugged her.

"I woke't up from earthquake but Dimitri no wake up. He dead by my side." Rita sobbed, unable to finish. Her tears poured as she collapsed, sobbing on Zoe's shoulder.

"So you all want to die?" hollered Sophia. "Tell that to Dimitri. Tell that to our dead and dying friends. Tell that to our ancestors. Tell that to—"

Without warning, Sophia stopped, wide-eyed, suddenly shockingly pale, clutching her left arm. She let out an agonizing grunt and began falling. Her daughter and Eleni bawled as Nikos managed to catch her in time, laying her gently on the ground. Sophia twitched and foamed at the mouth, her husband crying out for help. The navy chief surgeon and his men rushed to the scene and placed her on a stretcher.

"Take her to the infirmary!" he commanded.

Instinctively, Rita made a few steps toward the stretcher. She was still concerned for her best friend's well-being, even if Sophia was acting asinine. But Sophia being Sophia, and despite the fact that she was suffering from what appeared to be a heart attack, she kept lashing out.

"Hope you're all happy now!" she hollered, and gave Rita a venomous look. "I hope it was worth it. Rooting for her, and having a lover at your age… Shame on you!"

Rita cringed and returned the dirty look to her friend.

"Oh Sophia, drop dead already!" she bit back, finally and satisfyingly inflicting terror in the hawk woman's face.

As the stretcher disappeared through the crowd, Zoe turned and locked eyes with Paris.

"I'm so glad your face didn't crinkle up, and that you're actually close to my age, cousin. Haaa!" she joked, trying to break the ice. He grinned.

A desperate sea of faces now stood between them. Trapped by the throngs, the crowd swept the couple completely apart. In time, the families of the sick and dying got Paris' attention, while Zoe joined Claudia in escorting Rita to her home.

TWENTY-THREE
FOR SALE

The following day, a heavenly sun shined bright over six hastily built wooden caskets at the cemetery. There would have been more burials had the navy chief surgeon not insisted on performing detailed autopsies on all the deceased.

Rita, Zoe and Claudia followed the funeral service for Dimitri, both Father Michael and Paris, performing all six services together. Apart from the immediate families, there were no others in attendance.

"Where is everyone?" Zoe asked, looking around. She spotted Sophia sitting in a wheelchair at the edge of the cemetery observing the services with Nikos by her side. She had an oxygen tank at her feet, the tube running to a breathing mask over her face. Zoe almost felt sorry for her.

"The infirmary had eighteen new admissions today. Their families and friends are at their side. Many of them won't survive the week," Claudia explained to Zoe.

Father Michael looked older too, his graying beard all white now, his features more dignified than ever. He squinted as he chanted verses from the Bible while the navy personnel lowered Dimitri's casket into the grave with ropes, keeping the lid open as is the custom.

"Who's in the box? He looks handsome!" Rita wondered with a hint of a grin.

Zoe and Claudia looked at each other, acknowledging their sorrow for the woman who, by the dawning of this day, would fall hard into her diagnosed condition of dementia. She would also look at Zoe blankly, asking her repeatedly who she was.

After the funerals, the mourners followed Father Michael to Nikos' tavern for brandy and bitter biscuits. Claudia took charge of Rita and guided her along the path while Zoe and Paris stayed behind waiting for the mourners to disperse. Zoe gazed at him, running her fingers over his new stubble, up his sideburns and through his hair.

"What...?" he asked.

She frowned mockingly.

"Just some white hair, that's all..."

"So am I a little older than you thought?" he said smiling.

They walked a parallel path on the hump of the island, getting an overhead view of the village below. They said nothing for a while, afraid of ruining this peaceful moment where a slight sea breeze was all that whistled in their ears. He looked at her and broke the silence.

"How are you?"

She laughed.

"I'm alright... We surely made a mess of things."

"We've done nothing wrong."

"Even if *we're*—"

"On these islands, everyone's related to a degree."

"So we couldn't escape our fate?"

"Someone had to break the curse. Glad it was us. If this is what it took, then it must've been right..."

"I don't understand what you mean. Was this all a set up to break the spell? So you can free yourself of guilt for your mom's death?" Zoe questioned, her smile now gone.

"What about you, big city lady? Trying to make a fast dollar with Grandma's house only to run away?"

"Well yes. But that's before I finally found a sense of place, of... *home*."

They stopped walking. She looked at him, anxious about what he would say next.

"Petra was never for you. We both know this. You have the signed title deed now, so you can do as you please," he remarked.

Tears welled in her eyes. He immediately felt a fistful of guilt.

"What do you want from me?" he asked.

"Come back with me. Leave this all behind you..."

"I cannot. I've taken my vows."

"You can make a fresh new start. You can walk the city streets all night long. Nobody will know who you are, or where you come from. Be a priest, don't be a priest. I don't care. Just be... with... *me*."

"Do you see what's going on? They need me now more than ever. I caused all this and I'm responsible for them. The sick and dying are waiting to give me their last confessions as we speak. They're frozen with fear, knowing their end is near. I cannot abandon them..."

She fell on him fiercely, embracing him tightly, crying on his chest. He lifted her head and gave her a long, deep kiss. Then, gently, with the taste of her tears burning his lips, he broke the embrace and backed away.

"I must go," he said and turned his back to her.

"Wait!" she shouted and stopped him in his tracks. She ran next to him, unhooked the watch from her wrist and clasped it on his hand.

"Zoe, I don't—"

"She would have wanted you to have it. Besides, it works now, and I don't want it anymore. You'll need it more than me."

They looked at each other one last time before he descended the grassy hill toward the port. She watched him until he disappeared behind the first houses, then her tears stopped. She knew not why, but the crying was now over for her. Maybe it was these three hundred plus text messages on her smartphone, a piece of New York-ness claiming her back, a much needed balance to her over the top Greek-ness? Zoe just knew it was time for her to leave.

The villa had sustained minor damage and had lost some shutters, but that was the extent of it. Maria's home was still standing, which could not be said for many other homes on the island. Claudia was in the stateroom, looking up at the chandelier, when Zoe walked through the door. She noticed how really attractive the German woman looked considering her precipitous aging, her white hair hanging freely, covering her shoulders. They met under the light fixture and looked at each other waiting for the other to speak.

"I didn't have the right to buy this place, you know—" Claudia admitted.

"I know. So why'd lead me on?" asked Zoe.

"Sophia. She didn't want you on the island. And I knew she would do anything in this regard—even buy the villa.

So I wanted to drive up the price, so she would pay dearly for what she did to my uncle and your Yiayia..."

"Nice one. Well-played!" Zoe whooped.

"But there was also a risk you'd fall in love with the island and make it your home. Either way, Sophia would have been superbly livid, and all of Maria's and Stefanos' detractors would have failed. A win-win, any way you split it..."

Both ladies cracked the tiniest of smiles and blew humphs through their nostrils. They looked around the villa ruminating about the past and "what could have been" for the future.

"Part of me did want to buy it, however... For all the work I've put into solving the mystery of this island," the German woman dreamed, as she walked about examining the home. "And to exonerate my uncle and my family's name. Guess I felt I deserved it somehow. It almost feels without a purpose now. I'm sorry."

Zoe nodded.

"What will you do?"

"I want to see Germany again and see my family. But I'll return with some new research grants. The island still has a lot to reveal and its geological findings alone will fascinate scholars for ages. You?"

"I'm leaving for America. Time to go home, I guess."

"The frigate departs for Andoriani this evening. I can get you on the manifest—"

"That'd be great. All I have is a suitcase, all packed to go. Never did get to hang up my hat..."

Claudia backed toward the door.

"Departure is at 1900 hours, sharp—"

"I'll be there. How's Rita, by the way?"

"She's... *gone*. And she's not coming back."

Claudia turned and disappeared into the sunlight.

~

Surprisingly, Manos was up and about, managing his store. She found him behind the counter, gulping raki and wincing, completely unstoppable. This time, she didn't need to make a phone call. She had already texted Katie with her smartphone. She bought sandpaper, stucco, paint, varnish, a new lock, and some odd tools. By early evening, she would have her door fixed as new and would feel very proud about it. She also bought a "For Sale" sign that caused Manos to give her a knowing look.

"I don't feel one ounce of guilt," she stated.

"Ah ah, you'll be back," he retorted, smiling.

She hugged and kissed him regardless, just in case she never saw him again.

Zoe then walked all the way to Stefanos' house. Claudia had mentioned she would find a local resident to care for the place while she would visit Germany, and most importantly, to water her uncle's blooming carnations. Zoe took as many picture frames of her grandmother she could fit in her handbag.

~

Zoe affixed the "For Sale" sign on her door, and with a black marker, scribbled her email and phone number on it, along with the words: "Reduced Price" and "Make Offer" in bold lettering. With her suitcase at hand, she then hobbled down Petra's cobblestones toward the port. She paused for a minute at the square and surveyed the church. There was another funeral service in progress inside, and she could hear Paris chanting.

Some mourners who stood outside glared at her with hatred, while others just simply looked away. Zoe turned

224

and walked on, taking in the rapidly changing life of Petra.

Supply ships had been arriving to the island since dawn, carrying food, medical relief and engineers to repair the damaged infrastructure. The hustle and bustle in the port was intense. There were now two smaller navy ships moored along with the frigate. Greek and European officials were having a meeting at the port café, surrounded by journalists, distraught islanders and a bunch Petra's *guests*. Sitting on a pile of fishing nets was Aaron, all dressed in white linen and a straw hat. He was waiting for Zoe. He managed to push himself up with the aid of a cane and approached her with a small basket of figs. She was pleased to see that he looked remarkably handsome even in his advanced age.

"That for me?" she asked, as he offered her the basket.

"Heard you were leaving and I came to see you off. You, ma'am, are Petra royalty. And I needed you to know that. Your departure is our loss."

Zoe was instantly overcome with emotion. She gave Aaron a warm hug, releasing all her bottled up emotions.

"Petra still has its king," she replied, fighting back her tears.

The navy chief surgeon edged the ship's deck and motioned Zoe to hurry. Seamen busily pulled the ropes from the dock bollards. She gave Aaron a kiss and reached for the gangplank.

"I think I'm done with this place," she added, her lower lip shaking.

Aaron finger gunned her and grinned.

"Hey now... Don't be cruel!" he voiced, which made her entire face beam.

She marched up the plank and once she reached the deck, the navy chief surgeon was there to greet her.

"I am not yet convinced that what you did was illegal, interfering with a government investigation... I cannot say for sure that I will miss the way things were. Don't know if I should thank you or put you in the brig?"

He didn't bat an eyelid with his delivery, making Zoe respect his straight-laced wit.

"If you can just get me to Andoriani, I would be grateful," she said, equally serious.

He cracked a tiny smile as he stood aside, gesturing her in. A seaman took her suitcase and disappeared into the cargo hold. Zoe felt the navy frigate vibrate under her feet, the sea bubbling up with foam.

The ship sailed away fast, Petra immediately making distance with the stern. Zoe ran to the back railing and watched the setting sun as Aaron got smaller and smaller as he waved at her. Zoe then followed the railing all the way to the bow. About a week ago, Petra had greeted her, shrouded in mystery, as a puzzle and a promise. It took her in, gave her a Greek identity, and now was leaving her scarred and hurt. She was a bit too Greek, after all, as tears ran freely down her cheeks. She felt a tap on her shoulder and turned to join Claudia, who gave her an understanding look. Zoe needed that look more than anything else right now, and hugged the German woman hard, crying freely and unabashedly on her shoulder. When she looked back at the island, Petra was already a memory.

TWENTY-FOUR
GOODBYE

He took a few steps back to admire his work. He smirked as he reminisced. *"You should put the smaller clocks on the bottom and the bigger ones up top. Make it top-heavy. It'll make for a more striking perspective."* The clocks all ticked in unison, their dials in synch with the tower's clock. The display at the center of the narthex would create an impressive greeting for the arriving worshipers, he imagined.

"Your mom would be so proud," said Father Michael, fixing new eyeglasses on his nose.

"She was able to see it better than I could. And she was right!" Paris bragged.

"That one there, on the end... the time is off," his dad pointed.

"No. That's New York time. Plus, it's impolite to point in church. You should know that already, Father," his son snapped back.

Paris looked at his wristwatch. "Pethi Mou. Paris" was also set in New York time. The old priest felt his heart breaking alongside his son's. He placed his hand on Paris' shoulder.

"I'm sorry, son. It was I who was weak and pressured you into a life you didn't want. I took your choices away and—"

Paris turned and halted him with a stare.

"All that belongs to the past."

An old lady exited the temple, happy to see them both.

"Fathers..." she exclaimed, and proceeded to kiss their hands. She mostly clung onto Paris' hand.

"You're our comfort now, my *palikari*," she said, before stumbling out into the blazing sun.

"Alas," said Paris to his father. "It appears the stone has already been cast. It is therefore beyond our control."

"And I shall support you, no matter what you decide—"

"I have made my decision."

Father Michael hugged his son and fought back his tears.

"I'm going home to rest. I love you, I want you to know that. God be with you, my son."

They exited the church. Father Michael entered the house as Paris stayed to inspect the new scaffoldings. Masons from the mainland were busy making repairs to the bell clock tower. The whole of Petra was abuzz with new blood arriving to help the island get back on its feet. And families were also returning to their old homesteads with talks about reopening the old school.

Paris' eyes wandered to the piles of scaffolding debris next to the fig tree, his mind lost in memories. When all of a sudden, something waved him out of his fog; a piece of paper flapping in the breeze, wrapped around a wildly bent iron bracket. He approached the paper with great curiosity and untangled it carefully. To his surprise, it was the signed title deed to Zoe's villa. He smiled bitterly.

~

Paris climbed the cobblestone road through the village, carrying his handbag while observing images of Petra that he had never seen before. Or, that he may have forgotten. Cruise ships had begun docking at the port alongside the navy ships that kept bringing in supplies. The elderly residents of Petra—the ones that had survived—were the object of much attention, mainly for the benefit of science. Scientists and tourists from all around the world roamed the streets, snapping photos of them. But it was the local children that stirred the utmost nostalgia in Paris. He watched as a bunch of kids kicked a soccer ball around a field, remembering his good old days. He also noticed a few "To Let" signs on the doors of homes. He felt happy for Petra. But the island had been his prison all his life, and now—

"Good morning to you, Father!" called out a man riding past him on a mule.

The shackles were locked tight. He had a scared and needy parish that was setting high expectations for his youth and vows. They believed that it was Father Michael who had failed them for being unable to stop Sophia's wrath throughout the decades. Many still gathered at Sophia's, listening to her never-ending tirades and untruths. But for most islanders, Paris was now their new hope.

He paused outside a strange house and took his *kalimavki* (black head dress) out of his bag. He fitted it tightly to his head before knocking. It was Kostas' sister Irene who opened the door. She kissed Paris' hand and guided him to the backroom where Kostas waited on his deathbed. A navy doctor and her assistant sipped coffee at a small table in the hallway. Their part was now done.

The old man's eyes sparkled at the sight of the priest. He extended his mummified hand, desperately seeking comfort. Paris held Kostas' and smiled reassuringly. He then draped the ceremonial vestment around his neck and began chanting prayers. In bursts of small breaths, the old man gave his confession, admitting his basking in eternal life as his greatest sin. Paris offered Kostas holy communion and made the sign of the cross over him. A sweet, toothless smile made his shrivelled face beam with happiness. Kostas closed his eyes and sunk back in his pillow.

"O Master, Lord our God Almighty, who willest that all men should be saved and should come to a knowledge of the truth, who desirest not the death of a sinner, but that he should turn again and be saved: We pray thee and beseech thee, deliver thou the soul of thy servant Kostas from every bond, free it from every curse. For thou art he who delivereth them that are bound, and guideth aright them that are cast down, O Hope of the hopeless."

Paris was too choked up to say anything else. He left the house without uttering another word.

∼

He arrived at Zoe's villa, greeted by the "For Sale" sign plastered on its door. The place was unlocked. He walked in, hoping to meet Claudia, but she was nowhere to be seen. He removed a smartphone from his pocket and texted her. "12 o'clock?" he wrote.

Claudia had kept her promise to Zoe in maintaining her villa. The scent of fresh paint was strong in the state-room and drop sheets were covering the furniture once more. The haunting emptiness stung him badly, and for a moment, he felt unsure about all his decisions. He was then alerted by the buzz of his phone. "Coming!" Claudia replied.

Paris turned to leave when his exit was obstructed by an elderly couple who were checking out the place, their eyes wandering over the high ceilings. They were not locals, yet they looked very familiar, he thought.

"Excuse me, Father, are you the owner?" asked the old man.

"No, I'm not. The owner has gone back home."

"When will they return?"

"Never. Least not in this lifetime..."

The old man was ready to ask more questions, but Paris didn't care to listen. He excused himself and left, his stomach tied in knots. As he made distance with the villa, he remembered the old couple from Saint Peter's Day. It was the old rich man who flashed money to get his sick wife on Petra! Paris grinned. And in his mind, he wished them well.

By noon, the masons were taking their lunch break down by the pier. Paris had tipped them well for their earnest work and so they were treating themselves to some ice cold beers at the port café.

As he ascended the scaffoldings, Paris felt the fresh plaster of the tower. The dials and the numbers on the big clock gleamed a polished black under a new coat of paint.

He stood at the edge of a plank and gazed beyond the empty square toward the red rooftops of Petra. Somewhere, a mother was calling her son to come home for lunch. He remembered that the church was built on an ancient Greek temple devoted to the goddess of love. And wasn't love the cornerstone of Christianity? Humans keep busy erecting obstacles against their happiness all their lives —because of honor, duty, pride, legacy—and as a result, they make themselves suffer for nothing, turning their back to the only solution that can set them free... *love*. It's so simple and yet so difficult. He could not bear to betray the saddest of truths; serving people with blocked ears and hearts. Why suffer blindly when you can die for love, he thought. He stood at the edge and looked down. Claudia was late, but he didn't fret. She would take care of things. He was now free.

~

Father Michael sipped his coffee nervously and rubbed the tabletop with his knuckles. He stared at a picture frame on the wall, his soul burning with memories of his late wife, Catherine. He could still remember the sound of her soothing voice. And he never stopped longing for the feel of her skin, nor the smell of her hair.

Below the picture of Catherine was a photo of his boy, Paris. Lost in thought, he hoped it wasn't too late to make amends with his son. His lips curled with a sad smile.

Suddenly, a woman shrieked outside and Father Michael shot to his feet. Troubled voices began multiplying in the church square as the old priest darted out of his house. A desperate crowd surrounded the base of the bell clock tower. As the people parted, Father Michael made way to find Paris sprawled on the ground with Claudia kneeling over him. She looked up and Father Michael read the message in her eyes. His son was dead.

TWENTY-FIVE
AMERICAN DREAM

The Adirondack Amtrak train entered Penn Station late in the evening. It was raining, and it suited Zoe just fine. She considered New York City at its prettiest in mid-Autumn and as far as she was concerned, this here now, was her real homecoming. A month of curling up at her childhood home in Saratoga Springs and avoiding the world had worked its magical healing. Her father had welcomed her in with no questions asked. One morning, she sat up and told him the whole story, and he replied by saying it was time for her to head back to the city.

Katie had enough confidence to run the store on her own, but "Zoe's Blue Jeans Shoppe" would not survive for long without its owner. When it came to her business, there was too much of Yiayia Maria in Zoe's heart. From the day she returned from Greece, the reality of her life caught up with her in a vengeance. But recently, things were surprisingly looking up. The website miraculously helped boost the market value of the store. So much so that the bank was open to renegotiate the previous line of credit. The recent positive buzz kept her busy enough to push the island of Petra to the recesses of her mind. And it worked for a while. The September back-to-school rush came and went, and then that email from Eleni arrived. Zoe could not figure out how Eleni could have found her email address, but that wasn't important. The message revealed that Paris had died.

Numb from the shock, Zoe spent a torturous day trying to get in touch with anyone on Petra to confirm the news. She called and called and failed to reach Father Michael and Claudia. But she eventually got Manos in his store. And it was true. She heard the old man weeping on the other end. It was an accident, he explained. The young priest had fallen off the clock tower's scaffold. Zoe collapsed, fell apart, then fled the city seeking shelter under the covers of her childhood bedroom. She thought her mourning would never end. But now she was back, New York City was home, and it was time she started dealing with life again.

By the end of October, she had found herself back in full business mode. Katie was dropping hints about a partnership, and Zoe was not above considering an offer. Upon her initial return to the U.S., she was as close-lipped as a riddling sphinx to her assistant's incessant enquiries about what had transpired in Greece. But after her bereavement, Zoe shared everything with Katie over bagels and coffee. Curses, earthquakes, cousin relations and all. The one side effect was Katie joining the growing bandwagon of Zoe's friends who were trying to fix her up with a new nice young man. "Don't keep your bar so high! Greek gods don't really exist," Katie would repeat annoyingly. Zoe had promised to let her know when she felt she was ready. She had resisted the notion of dating again, despite the romantic charms of New York City in the Fall.

~

It was the last Saturday of October and they stayed late to take inventory of the new winter stock that had just arrived from their many suppliers. Katie was also busy setting up the window display, while Jeffrey was snapping photos for their website. They were hoping to finish counting and setting up their stock before it got too dark, then grab a late night bite at the pizza joint just around the corner. And already on display was their very own label of stone-washed blue jeans and other apparel made with the stones that Zoe had brought back from Petra. The clothing line was slowly gaining traction and earning commercial fame. Despite all the work that needed to get done, Zoe didn't shut down the store. She was never in the habit of turning away customers. Jeffrey was taking photos of garments that he had set up on the counter, while Zoe was dressing a mannequin with a new parka.

"Try one on!" Katie suggested. "And strike a pose on the sidewalk for Jeffrey?"

Jeffrey seemed to agree, but Zoe frowned.

"I'm not plastering myself all over the Internet, no thank you," she pronounced.

Zoe heard the door to the store open behind her, but she didn't turn around as she was too busy dressing the parka around the figurine.

"You got this?" she asked Katie, referring to the potential customer.

Zoe left the parka unbuttoned to showcase their new stone-washed jeans that the mannequin was wearing.

"Excuse me. Do you sell stone-washed jeans here?" said

the voice behind her. And that's when Zoe felt the floor vanish beneath her.

She turned around just to be 100% sure. Also, thinking she may have made a mistake. Zoe had never seen him in street clothes before and in blue jeans for that matter! She squeaked like a young thing, thunderstruck by his clean-shaven smile and his sea blue eyes. Resisting her primal urge to faint, she fell on him, hugging, kissing, punching, slapping and crying. All her sorrow and happiness expressed in a single explosion of emotions.

Paris wrapped her in his arms and she remained in his embrace, relieved and sobbing with abandon.

Katie quickly picked up on what was happening and that was enough for her eyes to swell up. Jeffrey had absolutely no clue what was going on. Still, his eyes grew wide.

"What da fuck! How could you do this to me! What the heck happened? How are you even alive, and—" Zoe sobbed all over his jacket.

"I know, I know... I'm so sorry," Paris pleaded, hugging her even tighter.

He smelled so much like autumn rain, and she wanted him all to herself. Zoe took Paris outside under the setting sun, to make sure he was actually real. She was beyond words, said nothing to Katie, the store instantly out of her mind. She held his hand tight, dragging him through the streets, unable to stop howling. They made a beautiful couple; Zoe a school-girl with a huge crush, Paris a culture-shocked boy who couldn't get enough of the big city vibe that cuddled them.

"I got on a plane! And I flew for the first time in my life... Can't believe how enormous this city is!" were some of Paris' random utterances during their sprint across Queens.

They eventually sat on a bench by the East River. She rested her head on his chest, her ear joyously listening to his heartbeat. And they said nothing, just watched the boats sail by until the sun set. Paris mentioned he was not staying at a hotel, that he was a guest in a Greek home, some distant relatives of his father. It was not that far away, so they decided they would go and get his stuff tomorrow. For tonight, he was staying with her. There were more pressing questions bubbling in Zoe's head, afraid he would slip again through her fingers like an illusion. His hand stroked her hair.

"I did die. With the help of Claudia and a very special potion that—"

"Old fig serum, which puts farm animals into deep sleep! No. I don't believe you!" She cracked up with laughter, and teasingly slapped his chest.

"Exactly. When you drink it, you fall into a coma, not unlike death. Of course, that alone was not enough for this priest to burn and rise like the phoenix. I had conspirators who went along with the plan... Like my poor father who agreed and performed my ceremony—"

"You mean your funeral?"

"Yes. Too bad I couldn't watch it. I was stone cold *dead*. They laid me in a coffin and buried me, too. Claudia and my father dug me out later and Dr. Patrikos managed to resuscitate me—"

"The navy chief surgeon?"

"He's the one that arranged for my passage off the island. Even got me a passport."

"Way to go Team Paris!" Zoe looked so pleased, but Paris mused a little.

"Though I'm now dead for everyone else on the island. Manos, Aaron, even Nikos..."

"You're telling me there's an empty grave with your name on it? That's fucken hilarious. I mean, morbid... but too funny—"

"Well, not exactly empty. We didn't want to leave the coffin empty, otherwise the weight of the soil would collapse into it, leaving people wondering—"

"I don't get what you're saying." Zoe looked confused.

"So we had to weigh it down... Remember that taxidermy sheep of Claudia's?"

"No, no. You lie—"

"I do not."

They both burst into hysterics. After a moment of gut-busting laughter, he lifted his sleeve to show her the Cartier wristwatch.

"And you forgot this."

"Does it still work?"

"Yes."

"Then I don't want it. It's yours."

The park lamps turned on, the vista of the city sparkled under a canopy of stars. In Zoe's imagination, Petra was there, just a bridge's distance from them.

"You know, I had a dream recently," she imagined. "That you and I were living on the island and that we were raising our children there... But now it can never be."

"It can still happen."

"How?"

"Petra is the place where miracles happen. Is it not?"

She rested her head on his chest and smiled.

"We'll see."

They would see, after they figured out the other pressing matter of: "*Now what?*"

For now, she cast her worries away. In her mind, they

had just met and things were looking up. And just like in the last shot of the movie, *The Graduate*, as Elaine and Benjamin sat on the bus looking straight ahead to an unknown future, Zoe thought that no matter what, it was going to be a beautiful and exciting ride.

THE END

Thinking about donating to a charity?
Please consider making a donation to your local
Huntington disease society.
Thank you!

Don't miss out on your next favorite book!

Join the Satin Romance mailing list
www.satinromance.com/mail.html

THANK YOU FOR READING

~

Did you enjoy this book?

We invite you to leave a review at your favorite book site, such as Goodreads, Amazon, Barnes & Noble, etc.

DID YOU KNOW THAT LEAVING A REVIEW...

- Helps other readers find books they may enjoy.
- Gives you a chance to let your voice be heard.
- Gives authors recognition for their hard work.
- Doesn't have to be long. A sentence or two about why you liked the book will do.

DINO HAJIYORGI

Dino Hajiyorgi was born in Istanbul in 1963 and lived in Chalkida, Greece. An award-winning writer, he was a film school graduate of ArtCenter College of Design in California, and worked as an animation series scriptwriter for Greek and German studios. An honorary member of the Athenian Club of Science Fiction, his short stories appeared in newspapers, magazines, anthologies, and in the Greek edition of Asimov's Magazine.

Dino's additional published books are: *Nighttime Traditions, Ashes on Marble, Wolf of the Sea,* and *Saltibango and the Cats of Hydra.*

https://www.facebook.com/theislandofzoe
https://www.facebook.com/dinos.hajiyorgis

CHRISTOS SOURLIGAS

Christos Sourligas is an award-winning and bestselling author and award-winning film-maker. He has created and produced multiple feature films and television shows, and as a former senior executive for several internationally-renowned television production companies, he's successfully brought shows into the homes of over 1.5 billion television viewers worldwide, airing in over 140 countries, and on 100 airlines. He also serves as a mentor and volunteer with various awards events, festivals and non-profit organizations. Christos resides in Montreal, Canada, and travels often to his ancestral home in Arcadia, Greece.

https://www.facebook.com/theislandofzoe
https://www.facebook.com/christos.sourligas.3
https://www.instagram.com/christossourligas/
https://www.onemanbandfilms.com

www.ingramcontent.com/pod-product-compliance
Lightning Source LLC
Chambersburg PA
CBHW022036240626
47154CB00007B/2440